MURUGA

MURUGA - THE WISE WARRRIOR

First edition. October 20, 2024.

Copyright © 2024 Arvind Seshadri.

ISBN: 979-8227706560

Written by Arvind Seshadri.

MURUGA

The Wise Warrior

Arvind Seshadri

Acknowledgement

I have traversed my journey of self-discovery over the last few years, unearthing my penchant for words both in the form of poetry and books, and here is another chapter in that journey. Growing up in a religious background and being initiated into spirituality quite early has helped me stay rooted during the ups and downs of my life.

This book is, in some ways, a tribute and homage to Lord Muruga. I have also written a few hymns about him in my mother tongue, Tamil. Muruga evokes a profound emotion of devotion in me, and I am enchanted whenever I visit any of his shrines. I feel the vibration and divinity in his temples. Hearing songs by the *Vaakyakaras* (great composers) like Muthuswamy Dikshitar, Periyasamy Thooran, Muthuthandavar, and Arunagiri Nathar triggers an immeasurable bliss within me, which can only be experienced and not described in words.

Having read all of Ashwin Sanghi's book, a genre I enjoy because of the beautiful blend of technology and tantra, covertness and culture, I was looking for more books to read, and while in conversation with a relative, she mentioned the Shiva Trilogy, a book I had always wanted to read but had missed out on. I chanced upon all three books bundled together at a bookstore and immediately bought them. A few chapters into the book, I was spellbound by the author's nuance and depth of knowledge. I was mesmerized by the humanization of Shiva. When I finished reading 'The Immortals of Meluha', a seed was planted in my mind that I should humanize one of the gods whom I relate to deeply, and immediately, Lord Muruga came to my mind.

Amish is the inspiration for this book, and I would like to convey my deepest gratitude to this wonderful author. He has probably inspired many budding authors with his masterpieces, which are selling worldwide. I am not a professional author, but someone trying to convey my thoughts and experiences through writing.

I would like to acknowledge my family: My wife Kavita and my children, Manisha and Niharika, who have been a constant support through my transformation from an upper middle-class management professional to an accidental author and poet by chance.

Last but not least, my wife's aunt, Usha Raghavachari, who is my go-to person for discussing religious, spiritual, and cultural matters. She was thrilled about my idea of writing this book. She supported me in many ways in writing this book. A big thank you to her, too.

NAADHA VINDHU KALADHEE NAMO NAMA
VEDHA MANTHRA SOROOPA NAMO NAMA
NYAANA PANDITHA SAAMEE NAMO
NAMA...VEGUKOTI

Salutations to the seed of Shiva and Shakthi
Salutations to the form that represents the Vedas
Salutations to the Lord of Wisdom
Salutations to the one with crores of names

Preface

Rama and Krishna, the two most revered gods of the Indian subcontinent, belong to the Vaishnavite sect of Hinduism. Much has been written and talked about them across India and the world, offering abundant life lessons from these two avatars. Although both were born in the North of India, their influence has mesmerized people globally. As a Vaishnavite, I am in awe of these avatars of Vishnu and the teachings they offer.

I am also a Tamilian, and in the South of India, we have our own avatar who is worshipped and revered not only in the southern peninsula but also in Sri Lanka and Malaysia. He is Muruga, fondly known as *Tamizh Kadavul, the God of the Tamils.*

Muruga's life is a tapestry of tantrums, frustration, love, courage, happiness, and evolution – experiences that resonate with all of us. An ardent lover of language, literature, and music, Muruga's devotees epitomize bhakti, particularly during *Thai Poosam,* a very sacred day for the *Kaumaris,* those who follow the path of Muruga.

Muruga belonging to the Shaivite sect as the son of Lord Shiva, has six abodes in Tamilnadu known as the *Arupadai Veedu,* where devotees flock throughout the year with their wishes. In Karnataka, the temple of Kukke Subramanya is considered a crucial shrine to visit for fulfilling one's desires. In Sri Lanka, the temple of Kathirgamam attracts scores of devotees, as do the Batu Caves near Kuala Lumpur, Malaysia, where there is a 100-foot Muruga statue. Archaeological surveys even suggest the existence of Muruga temples in the Middle East and Turkey. Despite his widespread worship, Muruga remains primarily a South Indian God, with few temples in the North of India. One notable exception is the temple in Uttarakhand, located 10,000 feet above sea level atop a mountain, where he is worshipped as Lord Karthik.

Muruga was born with a purpose, while Rama and Krishna found their purpose. Muruga evolves from a childhood with tantrums into a colossus. What if Muruga was a human who became deified due to his deeds? What would his life teach us today?

This book attempts to humanize Muruga, inviting readers to visualize his life and deeds, which could help in their own transformation. It is a blend of fiction and excerpts from the revered text of *Kandha Puranam,* the literature that depicts Muruga's life.

Table of Contents

List of Major Characters and Tribes
(In alphabetical order)

Adhi Veeran – Prince of Lanka Pattinam

Agni Mugan – Sooran's son

Ajamukhi – Sooran's sister

Amrutha – Muruga's Wife and Deva's daughter

Amothakan – Sooran's Interior Minister

Asurendra – The founder of the Asura Clan

Banukoban – Sooran's eldest son

Chandra – Muruga's foster father and Krithika's husband

Deva – The dethroned king of the Sura Clan

Dhanvantri – The chief physician of the Sura Clan

Gaja Mugan – Guardian of eastern gate of Mahendrapuri

Hiranyan – Sooran's son

Indiran – Tharakan's son

Jayanthan – Deva's son held captive by the Asuras

Kamala – Muruga's Aunt

Krithika – Muruga's surrogate mother

Kashyapa – The great sage living in North India

Madan – The greatest sorcerer in the Sura clan

Mangalakesi – The first queen of the Asura clan

Maragathavalli – Senguntha's mother

Maya – Sooran's mother

Muruga – The wise warrior and son of Swayambhu

Padmakomalai – Sooran's wife

Pawan – Close aide of Deva and Muruga's charioteer

Prajapathi – Rajaguru of all the clans

Prajwal – The carrier of the energy core enabling Muruga's birth

Rishabha – Swayambhu's personal assistant

Rishiraja – The revered saint worshipped by all the clans

Sachi – Deva's wife

Senguntha – Muruga's best friend and commander

Shakthi – Swayambhu's wife and mother to Muruga

Shukra – The Guru of the Asura Clan

Simhan – Sooran's brother

Sooran – Asura King also known as Padman

Sowri – Tharakan's Wife

Sundara – Shakthi's brother

Swayamabhu – The supreme lordship of all the clans

Tharakan – Sooran's brother
Vajrabahu – Sooran's youngest son
Valli – Muruga's wife
Vignesh – Muruga's elder brother
Vishwakarman – The chief architect and engineer of the Suras

BREAKING THE PENANCE

(Circa 3100 BCE, Southern Kailash)

In the midst of the gloomy looking skies of Southern Kailash, Swayambhu was in penance. For ordinary yogis, penance was a means to an end but for the Maha Yogi with no beginning or end, it was a reflection of inner peace attainable through Yoga Nidra or Yogic sleep. He was demonstrating this to his students who were in front of him, they were the children of Prajapathi.

Swayambhu was teaching them the essence of the Vedic Scriptures and explaining to them the concept of *bhogam, enjoyment* and *yogam, control over body and mind*. Who better than him to teach! He was both an ascetic and a family man. Swayambhu, the head of the Gana Tribe was a multifaceted individual - Warrior, Yogi, Dancer all rolled into one. He was the Lord of the Ganas, the protector of the Suras, a wealthy tribe with abundant riches, wine and women. He was also the Supreme Lord for the dreaded and powerful Asuras.

Ever since Shakthi left to perform penance as a yogini seeking an ascetic life, away from the power filled Velliangiri, Swayambhu decided to embrace the yogi within him too. Before entering his trance, Swayambhu instructed his trusted lieutenant, Rishabha, to ensure that he wasn't disturbed as he would be in the state of yogic sleep.

'Do not let anyone in, except Madan,' said Swayambhu. Madan was the most famous sorcerer in the land.

Far away, Deva, the leader of the Sura tribe, anxious after losing his kingdom and son was engaged in an animated conversation with Prajapathi. Jayanthan, Deva's son was captured by the powerful Banu who was from their opposing clan the Asuras.

Prajapathi was responsible for maintaining the scriptures and teaching them to the different clans, he was from a sect called the Brahmans, whose charter was to read, understand and disseminate the wisdom of the scriptures.

Prajapathi's role was that of the Chief Priest of all the clans and a close confidant of Deva.

'Deva, speak to Swayambhu about your problem and seek a solution,' said Prajapathi.

Swayambhu is in penance and wouldn't want to be disturbed, how do we break it,' asked Deva.

Let's speak to Madan to conjure up something to awaken Swayambhu, even the great Vishwamitra's penance was broken by Menaka,' replied Prajapathi.

Deva sent word through one of his guards to go and fetch Madan. The guard left immediately and returned after a while with Madan.

'You summoned me Sura Pathi,' asked Madan referring to Deva as the leader of the Suras.

Prajapathi spoke about his plan to Madan who was taken aback. He was in a state of dizziness.

'You are asking me to go on a suicide mission. I have a family to take care of, please find someone else,' retorted Madan.

'Even if you had to sacrifice your life, it is for a greater good,' justified Prajapathi.

Prajapathi went on to give the example of Aravan, Arjuna's son who gave up his life for pandavas to win the war.

Madan knew he had to face the wrath of Deva or Swayambhu. He felt, if this was his fate, then he would rather face the wrath of the Supreme Lordship and die at his hands, which would be more befitting.

Summoning all his courage, Madan arrived at Velliangiri, determined to break Swayambhu's penance despite the risks. He saw Rishabha standing in the portico, he told Rishabha he had been assigned a task by Deva and Prajapathi and needed to meet Swayambhu.

'Something doesn't add up, anyway Lord Swayambhu asked me to only let you in and no one else, so go ahead,' said Rishabha.

Face to Face with Swayambhu, Madan prepared to cast his spell when Swayambhu opened his eyes. Madan could see the rage of Swayambhu in his eyes. The Maha

Yogi had been woken up and he was about to teach him a lesson, just then Rathi, Madan's wife ran in. She had followed Madan fearing that something untoward could happen. She begged Swayambhu to forgive Madan.

'Rathi, he needs to be punished for his sin,' said Swayambhu seething with rage.

'I banish him forever from all the kingdoms.'

'He will have to remain only in your sight and not show himself anywhere. Leave now!' said Swayambhu scornfully.

With Madan not returning, Deva and Prajapathi feared the worst. Now they had no other way but to present themselves before Swayambhu who had come out of his penance.

As Prajapathi and Deva were entering the courtyard, 'You guys always find scapegoats, don't you? You are spineless,' said an angry Rishabha.

Seeing both Prajapathi and Deva together, Swayambhu smiled.

'Looks like something very important, two stalwarts together,' said Swayambhu sarcastically.

Deva prostrated before Swayambhu.

'Oh Lord! you have a view of the past, present, and the future. We are doomed because the Asura clan is at its peak with my kingdom and my son gone. You are in ascetic state not worrying about anything that is happening in the world. We have only you to reach out,' lamented Deva.

'Deva, you are talking like a child,' Swayambhu chided him.

'Balance of power is required so that there is stability. Too much of your Somras is also poison, isn't it? Asuras also treat me as their de facto chief; how can I take sides?'

'One child is obsessed with wealth; the other child is obsessed with power. I can only step in when one side goes overboard so that equanimity can be restored,' concluded Swayambhu.

Deva intervened, 'pardon my Lord but we all feel if Shakthi was by your side, you would probably take a different view.'

'Deva, you are looking at things only physically that's why you don't see Shakthi,' retorted Swayambhu.

Shakthi never leaves me, she always drives me from within. Without Shakthi there is no Shambo, without Shambo there is no Shakthi.'

'Everything has a time and place and soon enough the Asura clan will see a downturn when they reach the tipping point. You need to wait patiently and not do anything impertinent till then. Because of your foolhardiness, Madan has been punished,' concluded Swayambhu.

Prajapathi swallowed his saliva, knowing very well that the chastening was for him too.

Meanwhile, down at the tip of the Indian ocean. Shakthi was doing her own penance, praying to Mahadev, oblivious to all the happenings in Velliangiri. Little did she know that her penance would also be broken soon. As she was meditating, she felt a strong heat generating on her forehead, she had a vision of Mahadev. She was shocked to see Swayambhu's face on Mahadev. She startled and opened her eyes. Realization had dawned on her that everyone was a manifestation of Mahadev. She remembered the saying '*Har Har Mahadev*'. She was Mahadev and so was Swayambhu.

As she opened her eyes, she saw a king and queen, prostrate in front of her, she raised them up and said she was a tribeswoman and a sadhu, being elders they should not be prostrating before her. The King introduced himself and his wife as Malayaman and Meena.

'You resemble Devi Kumari, a manifestation of Lord Parvathi whom we revere and worship here,' said Malayaman.

Shakthi closed her eyes and said '*Har Har Mahadev*' to herself.

'All of us are manifestations of Lord Mahadev, we all have a purpose to fulfil,' said Shakthi.

'Where are you from and why are you here?' asked Malayaman.

'I am Shakthi, I am from the Gana tribe, I am from Velliangiri, I live with my son Vignesh and husband Swayambhu who is the clan leader,' replied Shakthi.

'Nice to know, why choose this place for a penance,' asked Malayaman.

'I decided to become an ascetic to find the true meaning of life away from my powerful position and hence my trek to the tip of the Indian Ocean,' replied Shakthi.

'We will be honoured, if you stay for a few days with us,' said Malayaman.

'I have found realization in this region, your kingdom is truly blessed, the honour is mine,' replied Shakthi.

Shakthi stayed in Malayaman's palace for a couple of days and expressed her desire to go back to her kingdom.

'Shakthi, can I ask you something?' said Malayaman.

'You are like a father to me, please tell me what can I do for you? said Shakthi.

'We are very intrigued by your Kingdom and would like to take you back to Velliangiri in our chariot, and we look forward to meet your family too,' said Malayaman.

Shakthi was overjoyed. 'It would be my honour to host you and the queen,' said Shakthi.

Malayaman made the necessary arrangements for them to travel to Velliangiri, which literally meant the Silver Mountain and was the very reason it was called the Southern Kailash.

THE REUNION

A pigeon courier landed on the porch of Swayambhu's abode in Velliangiri. As usual Rishabha received it. He opened the palm leaf manuscript to read the contents, and a beaming smile swept across his face. The queen was returning home. He rushed in to inform Swayambhu, that the queen was coming home with a few guests as well. Swayambhu gave a wry smile, heart of hearts, he was brimming with joy to see his better-half returning home. He called Vignesh and told him to ensure that she gets the best welcome from her beloved son. After all, she was his creator and had a special affinity towards him. He ordered Rishabha to inform the Ganas and make the necessary arrangements for the guests who were coming.

The news spread like wildfire and it reached not only the Ganas but the Suras and the Asuras too. Deva was probably the one most pleased with the news, as he believed that Swayambhu would definitely find a solution to his troubles now that Shakthi would be beside him. Prajapathi informed about the homecoming to Sundara, who was Shakthi's brother and he was overwhelmed with joy too. He asked his wife Kamala to mark this occasion as a *griha pravesam, homecoming* and to ensure that it was a memorable one.

Deva and Prajapathi reached the house of Sundara with a plan. Sundara welcomed both of them to his abode named Vaikunta, a place of unending prosperity. Deva explained to Sundara that it was important for Shakthi to never leave Swayambhu again and to remain in marital bliss. He said it was good for her and all the tribes, as Swayambhu would remain a family man and spend time solving the problems of his people. Sundara interjected and said 'they are already married so what is your point?

'Let's perform the marriage ritual once again, as both of them have left their ascetic nature and are reuniting. People pray to Lord Rama and Sita by performing marriage ceremony for them, why not do it for Swayambhu and Shakthi who are revered by us,' said Deva.

Sundara thought for a second and said 'If it pleases you and the Ganas, I am happy to do the *kanya dhan, giving away the bride*, once again.'

Deva and Prajapathi were overjoyed and returned back to their respective abodes. Deva's abode was named *Swarga, heaven* and Prajapathi's humble abode was named *Sathya, truth*. Both the names reflected their life and lifestyle.

A day had passed and the entourage consisting of Malayaman, Meena and Shakthi entered the outer gates of Velliangiri. Malayaman was mesmerized by the beauty of the mountains and the serene atmosphere. Meena had developed a motherly affection towards Shakthi, and to see the place that she lived, filled her eyes with tears of joy. The Ganas blew the trumpet and made the typical rhythmic sounds unique to the Gana tribe to welcome their beloved queen. Vignesh was at the gate, eager to see his mother. Shakthi jumped out from her chariot in which Meena was also seated and rushed to hug her son. She had almost lost him once in a skirmish that had happened between Swayambhu and him. It resulted in Vignesh's face to be disfigured and he had to always wear a mask. Those memories flooded Shakthi's mind. Vignesh was a very cultured and wise boy, as soon as he saw Malayaman and Meena get down from their chariot, he bent down and touched their feet to get their blessings. Malayaman and Meena were overwhelmed with emotion to see the devotion and love that Vignesh had towards his mother and elders. Malayaman embraced Vignesh and said '*Chiranjeevi Bhava', may you be immortal.*

The tour party was taken by Rishabha to the guest quarters to get some rest and freshen up after a long journey. After a couple of hours Rishabha turned up at the guest quarters to take Malayaman and Meena for lunch at the house of his Lord, Swayambhu. The Gana tribe were staunch non-vegetarians, Lord Swayambhu and his family however were animal lovers. Swayambhu had a pet snake named Vasuki. It was around his neck most of the time. Ganesh had a pet mouse whose name was Mooshik and Shakthi had a lion named Dhawan, which she had nurtured since it was a baby. The lunch had a mix of fruits and vegetables and meat specially made for the royal guests. Shakthi had informed that there should be sweet modak for dessert, a favourite dish of Vignesh that she often made for her dear son. Both royal families enjoyed the feast along with special invitees Sundara and Kamala.

As twilight descended on Velliangiri, the place was lit with wooden lamps across the palace and combined with the moon light, it created a festive atmosphere. Prajapathi walked in with Vani and Deva arrived with Sachi, both of them were greeted by Swayambhu and Shakthi. They were introduced to the guests as well. After the pleasantries, Deva and Prajapathi put forth their plan of having a replica of their Lord's marriage ceremony, now that Shakthi had come back. Swayambhu didn't quite believe in these extravagances but they were after all his near and dear ones. When Vignesh, Sundara and Rishabha all shouted with joy on hearing this idea, Swayambhu and Shakthi relented and agreed for the mock wedding in the morning.

Hearing the news, the place was brimming with happiness and to match the mood, Rishabha started playing his drums which he called the 'Mridanga'. Vani soon joined in with her string instrument called 'Vana', she was a maestro and soon the musical jamming became so enthralling that natural dancers Swayambhu and Shakthi couldn't sit quiet, they joined the rhythmic beats and music with their dance steps and expressions. During the month of *chitthirai* of the Hindu calendar there was a great festival to celebrate Lord Mahadev and Goddess Parvathi and one of the most awaited performances was that of Swayambhu and Shakthi. Both complemented each other.

Swayambhu's speed with Shakthi's grace. It was known as *Lasya Tandavam, graceful dancing.* Velliangiri wore the look of an enchanted place amidst the music and dance which went through the night.

The Sun rose earlier than usual to be part of the festivities to mark the reunion of Swayambhu and Shakthi. The Mahadev temple had been chosen for the auspicious ceremonies and there were garlands and *thoranams, decorations* all across the temple. It had been a while since Velliangiri had seen any ceremony of this nature. Swayambhu's house wore a festive look too with colourful *kolams, decorative designs* in the portico and *ma-ilai, mango leaves* dangling in the front door. Vani and Kamala had arrived early at Velliangiri to get Shakthi decked up with traditional jewels and a hairdo to reflect the occasion. Kamala after all was her sister-in-law. Vani was well versed with the rituals associated with marriage. She ensured all the necessary items were available and in place. She didn't want any disruption especially during the *homam, sacrifice to the supreme via Agni, the god of fire,* or in the *poojai, rituals.*

Prajapathi donned the role of the priest to conduct the rituals for the king and queen. The bride to be, was taken in the chariot along with Malayaman and Meena. Rishabha was the best man and he along with Swayambhu left for the temple from their house by foot, the marriage party walked on the streets with the bridegroom and best man in tow. All the Gana tribe's men, women and children showered flowers and welcomed both the bride and the groom. The Suras led by their leader Deva, had also come in huge numbers to witness the magnificent wedding. Yogis who were performing penance for Lord Shiva had also come to bless the couple.

The temple was filled with everyone from the common man to yogis and warlords. Vedic recitals were being done by the Brahmans on one side and the Yogis on the other side. The atmosphere was reverberating with lilting rhythmic sound of the Vedic verses. When the *muhurtham, auspicious hour* had come, Prajapathi summoned Sundara to perform the act of *kanya dhaanam,* giving away his sister in marriage to the bridegroom. With the musical drums at their crescendo, Sundara placed the hands of his sister on Swayambhu's hand and entrusted the responsibility of Shakthi to him once again.

'Let there be only tears of joy in my beloved sisters' eyes,' he said.

The most important thing in weddings was the food. From fresh fruits to three course main meal, followed by sweets was something everybody looked forward too. There was a *mandapam* in the outer portion of the temple which had been converted to the dining hall. Vignesh was given the charge of the dining hall to ensure that not a single soul went home with an empty stomach. He had made necessary arrangements for people to be seated so that the cooks could serve the food in sequence.

Swayambhu was fond of milk, hence milk based sweet dishes were the order of the day that included *pedas, payasam etc.* There was also special dish called *pancha amritam* literally translating to five nectars. A concoction made from curd, milk, sugar, honey and ghee. It was considered the drink of the gods. It was such an irony that a huge portion of that was made and served to the common people of Gana tribe. They were blessed to have this dish perhaps the first and only time they would ever get to experience it. All the guests not only had their stomach full but also their hearts were filled with happiness. 'Long Live Swayambhu and Shakthi,' they shouted in chorus as they retreated to their respective households.

It was the custom that the bride and groom ate last. Swayambhu was happy with his usual milk and *pancha amritam,* which was his favourite sweet too. Shakthi was too exhausted and took the milk sweets and asked Vignesh to not leave anything behind and to eat everything. Vignesh never needed a second invitation when it came to food, he enjoyed eating the sweets and gorged on all that he could get his hands on, it was like an elephant running through the cane field with gay abandon. The reunion became etched in the memory of everyone who had been part of it. In the evening Swayambhu and

Shakthi bade farewell to their guests Malayaman and Meena and returned to their quarters after a tiring but fulfilling day.

QUEST FOR ANSWERS

It had been three weeks since the reunion of Swayambhu with Shakthi and Deva grew restless. He expected that Swayambhu would focus on solving his problems now that Shakthi was by his side. However, he noticed that Swayambhu appeared more focused on his family rather than addressing his concerns. Deva couldn't confront Swayambhu as he feared facing his wrath. He went back to his trusted partner, Prajapathi, to vent about his problems and seek his suggestions.

It was early evening when Deva reached *Sathya*, the abode of Prajapathi, to meet him. Prajapathi was in the midst of his *sandhyavandanam* which literally translates to 'salutations during twilight', a ritual that he practiced as a Brahman and was supposed to do it three times a day. After finishing his rituals, Prajapathi greeted Deva and they sat down in his chamber. Prajapathi offered Deva buttermilk, a customary gesture of hospitality.

'Prajapathi, you are well aware of my problems and I am still waiting for answers to them,' said Deva, rubbing both his palms together and pacing the room, engulfed in desperation.

'My kingdom is gone; my son is held captive and I am living a secluded life. With Shakthi's return, I hoped Swayambhu would become more worldly and focus on resolving my problems.

He seems to be completely oblivious to it and focused on his own family.'

'What do I do? Where do I go? Tell me, Tell me!' yelled Deva in a fit of rage and frustration.

Prajapathi, as always calm and composed, said, 'Deva, calm down, you are the leader of the Suras. If you show so much frustration and helplessness, it would demoralize and demotivate the entire clan.'

'Haven't I told you earlier? The only one who can find a solution, and will find a solution, is Swayambhu and no one else,' said Prajapathi firmly.

Prajapathi pointed to a palm leaf script and continued,

'I have gone through your horoscope, it shows your bad time, it also revealed that your good time will come soon, with the help of a warrior. We could go back to Swayambhu again with this additional information and hope that he provides a solution.'

Deva was starting to see light at the end of the tunnel.

Since it was a Tuesday, Prajapathi told Deva that it was an inauspicious day for travel, and they could travel tomorrow to Velliangiri.

It was Wednesday morning. Deva rose earlier than usual; he couldn't sleep the whole night as he kept replaying in his mind what Prajapathi had told him. He had learnt from the scriptures that there was nothing better than a Wednesday to start something new. Dressed in pure white and taking milk sweets along with him, he reached Prajapathi's house, who was ready and waiting. Prajapathi always got up very early at *brahma muhurtham*, the most auspicious time of the day to do his prayers. As the chariot rolled along the lush greenery on either side, Deva breathed the earthy scent and felt a sense of optimism.

Deva being a rich man, had enough wealth, even though he had lost his kingdom. He came to pick up Prajapathi in a chariot driven by elephants, a rare sight when most chariots were driven by horses. Both friends left for Velliangiri, hoping to end all uncertainties that surrounded the Sura clan. It wasn't a long journey, so they reached the doorstep of Velliangiri soon. At the entrance, they were greeted by the inimitable Rishabha.

'Namaskaram, Rishabha, we seek an audience with the Lord,' said Prajapathi.

'We have come to discuss a matter of grave concern,' said Deva.

Rishabha took the news to his Master. Swayambhu was wondering why both of them landed early in the morning with some issue. Shakthi enquired if all was well. Swayambhu asked Rishabha to escort them in. Both paid their respects to the Lord of Lords and his queen, who were seated on the throne.

'Oh Lord, I reach out to you again seeking solace for my troubles. Need you to help me with a solution to retrieve my kingdom and release my son,' said Deva with anguish and anxiety.

Shakthi looked at Swayambhu with a quizzical expression on her face.

'Oh, Deva!' said Swayambhu, with anger raging in his eyes.

'I have told you already that I have given my word to the Asuras that no harm would come to them directly from me.'

Prajapathi intervened and said, 'Dear Lord, I understand your predicament hence I have brought Deva's horoscope along with me. I request you to see it and then provide us with your solution and the way forward.'

Swayambhu nodded in acceptance and Prajapathi opened the scroll and showed the planetary positions of Deva and pointing out that in the near future there would be a change for the good and it would happen with the help of a warrior.

'You are the greatest of warriors. Astrology seems to be pointing out that you are the saviour, my Lord,' said Prajapathi.

In those times, whether King or common man, everyone believed in astrology.

Swayambhu thought for a moment and then said, 'I do agree that for centuries our clans have strongly believed in astrology but warrior doesn't mean only me. There were warriors before me and there would be warriors after me. While Vignesh has the ability to be a great warrior, he has chosen the path of wisdom and is sought out by people of all the clans to solve their problems using his wisdom. It is obvious to me that Vignesh can't help Deva. It could possibly be another son from our clan.'

'I do believe in astrology, if it says a warrior would be the saviour, there is some merit to it. Let me ponder over it. Till then, accept your current reality and be patient till the tide turns,' concluded Swayambhu.

As late evening approached and Swayambhu watched the sun setting behind the Velliangiri mountains, he was in a pensive mood. He was bound by his commitment to the Asuras but failing in his duties towards the Suras, who also considered him the Supreme Lord. With the indication from Deva's horoscope that it would be a warrior who would restore normalcy to the Suras, who would that be? where would he come from? These questions were eating at his mind.

Shakthi had silently walked behind him and touched his shoulders.

'It's not great to see you in despair. You are the Lord of Lords. Life always finds a way; we just don't know it yet. If you are engrossed in the problem, you will never find a solution to anything. You are a Gnani and a Yogi; you will find answers in your meditation. Mahadev has always answered everyone's call, he will answer yours too.'

'I will pray to Mahadev, and you meditate on him. Cut out the noise in your head,' she said hugging Swayambhu passionately. It was as if the earth and sky had come together and made everything else go out of context.

Swayambhu's mind became calm and composed after the non-verbal communication with Shakthi. After the early dinner, he went to sleep.

Swayambhu was sitting in front of a Shiva Lingam and a blinding light rose from it. Behold, Mahadeva was in front of him, pointing to his third eye on his forehead. Within seconds the flash disappeared. Swayambhu woke up startled. He looked around to see Shakthi sleeping like a child. He didn't understand the vision he had just experienced. *'It is a sign,'* Swayambhu thought to himself. He drank some water and went back to sleep.

The next morning, he woke up with vigour.

As he was having the morning breakfast with Shakthi and Vignesh, he looked at Shakthi and said, 'Mahadev has answered even before I sought him out.'

'You are a blessed soul,' said Shakthi.

Swayambhu quickly finished his breakfast and retreated to his quarters, and requested not to be disturbed. Swayambhu started to look for the palm leaf manuscripts that were written by sages and had been passed to him through his forefathers. He was specifically looking for a manuscript that talked about *'Kundalini'* energy. Interestingly it was referred to as *Kundalini Shakthi*. It was believed to be the most potent form of feminine energy, equivalent to the most powerful male energy called Shiva, the other name of Mahadev.

Swayambhu started reading about the *Kundalini Shakthi* and Energy Centre's called *Chakras* in the human body. He was looking at the process of activating each chakra within him and then aggregating them to create a powerful energy core. This energy core would be the culmination of Shiva, the masculine energy that represented the cosmic consciousness, and Shakthi the feminine energy that represented the cosmic potency. Mahadev had shown him the way; he now understood the vision he had seen earlier.

The family man was back to his ascetic nature; he shut himself out from the noise and started meditating deeply. No one dared to disturb him in anyway, lest they be banned for life like Madan. He was trained in meditation and yoga from a very young age, so for him it was like switching a button to get into this mode.

Days passed and the deep trance continued. After a week's time, Swayambhu felt a throbbing in the middle of his temple. The throbbing got heavier as days progressed and by the end of the second week, the throbbing had reached its peak. Swayambhu felt light and heat in the middle of his forehead. He knew he had reached the pinnacle of his *tapas, penance* and now he was ready with the solution. When the problem is complex, the solution can't be simple.

Swayambhu finally emerged from his self-imposed exile and returned to his beloved and his son. Shakthi was happy to see him. Swayambhu hugged her as a gesture of gratitude, as she had shown him the way. He sat next to Shakthi holding her hand and told her about the divine vision of Mahadev, which had led him to this hibernation for the larger good.

Swayambhu told Rishabha to set up an exclusive meeting with Deva, Prajapathi, Shakthi and himself to discuss a very important matter. The outcome of this meeting could change the course of the Sura clan forever. It was going to be the day of reckoning and probably provide an answer to the question of who the warrior would be.

SWAYAMBHU'S PLAN

Assembled in the courtroom, all the stakeholders were ready to listen intently to Swayambhu's speech, especially Deva, who waited with bated breath, as this was a day of reckoning for the Suras.

'Let me outline my plan to you. Over the last couple of weeks, I have been working on channelizing my *Chakras* to create a hyper energy system that would aggregate in the *Ajna Chakra,* located in the middle of the forehead between my eyebrows. This energy core would have to be transferred to an object worthy of carrying it. The object would have to be immersed in a sacred river to consecrate it and eventually be handed over to a recipient who can absorb this energy core into her womb. The energy core would then manifest itself into a human, who would possess immense power and become a *maveeran, great warrior,*' concluded Swayambhu.

There was pin-drop silence in the room. This was an intriguing plan but had many pieces of the puzzle that had to fall in place for it to work.

'I know you are all thinking about the different pieces of the puzzle. I have my thoughts, but would like to hear from you as well,' said Swayambhu.

Prajapathi, being the most learned man in the courtroom stood up and joined his hands in a Namaste.

'O Lord, let me give you my views on who could be the best person to carry this energy field to the river basin. The name that immediately comes to my mind is Prajwal. He plays with fire, is a fire breather and can withstand the strong heat emanating from the energy core. He is respected by the Sura community and always leads from the front,' said Prajapathi.

An excited Deva jumped into the conversation and said, 'I am in complete agreement with Prajapathi.'

'Prajwal is the most suitable person for this sacred task and the one whom I would entrust my life with. Prajwal would do anything for the clan and its future. I will ask Pawan to accompany him. He is his best friend and between the two of them, they will be able to accomplish this task,' concluded Deva.

Swayambhu was pleased with the direction the conversation was going. He had already made up his mind about Prajwal; he just wanted to hear from the people who were involved. His job was made easy with both Deva and Prajapathi proposing his name, he nodded his head in agreement to the proposal. With consensus reached on the first issue, the path forward became clearer.

The critical part still remained unanswered: who would carry the energy core in the womb? Deva and Prajapathi were deep in thought.

'I have a proposal for you all,' said Shakthi as all heads turned towards her.

Please go ahead, we are happy to listen to you,' said Swayambhu.

'You are aware of my half-sister Krithika, who lives in Poigai. She and her husband Chandra are childless as she hasn't been able to conceive. The energy core created by Swayambhu would be powerful enough to manifest itself; it just needs a *garba graham, a womb* to rest itself on. Given the magnitude of the task involved, I believe she would be a right candidate. She is an ardent devotee of Mahadev too,' concluded Shakthi.

'I will ask Chandra to come over. We can discuss the matter with him and take his consent,' said Swayambhu.

'I will send a pigeon courier to Krithika. I am sure she would be the happiest person on earth to hear this news,' said Shakthi.

There was a stunned silence in the court room; this was completely unexpected.

Swayambhu trusted Shakthi's instinct as his own. After all they were two different people with the same soul. Deva did not dare to open his mouth in front of Shakthi, it didn't matter how the objective was achieved as long as it was achieved.

Deva put his arms together in prayer pose and said 'You are our *matha,* whatever you say is a command for us,' referring to Shakthi as their mother.

Prajapathi, with a smirk on his face, said, 'After all, it's another Shakthi, who will beget the warrior. The Suras are blessed. I also approve of the solution, my lady.'

'Deva, go and brief Prajwal and Pawan on the sacred task at hand,' said Swayambhu and gestured for him to leave.

Deva bowed as a mark of respect and left immediately. As soon as he reached Swarga, he sent a messenger to Prajwal and Pawan's abode to summon them for a meeting.

Prajwal and Pawan stayed close to each other. Pawan always fueled Prajwal's ambitions. He quickly reached Prajwal's house.

'Why are we both being called together?' asked Pawan. Prajwal raised his arms in the air, a gesture to say that he didn't know.

'It must be something extremely important. Let's go without any further delay,' said Prajwal.

Pawan had horses that travelled the fastest in the kingdom. He rode with one and brought the other with him. The two friends mounted the horses and rode away with a strong tail wind behind them, reaching Swarga in no time.

Deva was in his portico, walking up and down. The moment he heard the neighing of horses, he knew the two prominent members of the Sura clan had arrived. He was all smiles and greeted them both. After exchanging pleasantries, Deva gave them a rundown of the entire plan that Swayambhu had conceived. Prajwal was pleased that he was chosen for this honour by all the revered members.

'Lord Deva! It is indeed a great honour for me to do something that would help my clan regain its past glory. I am sure Pawan is as eager as I am,' said Prajwal.

'I will support Prajwal to achieve the task assigned, just like Lakshman did for Sri Ram,' said Pawan.

'Let us know when we have to leave,' said both in unison.

'Lord Swayambhu will decide that. You both go and meet him in person at Velliangiri and seek his blessings,' said Deva.

It was now late in the evening. Swayambhu and Shakthi were in their quarters.

'*Swami,* I have to ask you a question about your plan. May I?' said Shakthi, referring to Swayambhu has her lord.

'*Priye,* you don't have to seek my permission for asking anything,' said Swayambhu, referring to her as his beloved.

'We discussed various aspects of your plan today, but what would be the object that would hold the aggregated energy of your Kundalini Shakthi? You didn't mention it in the discussions today,' said Shakthi.

'*Priye,* would I have not told you and the others had I known,' said Swayambhu with a smile on his face.

'The whole sequence of events seemed to be driven by the supreme divine force. Mahadev has shown me the way thus far, he will provide me the answer to the missing piece of the puzzle too,' said Swayambhu.

Just before going to sleep, Swayambhu closed his eyes and chanted 'Om Namah Shivaya' silently.

"Om Hreem Kleem Namaha, Om Hreem Kleem Namaha"

The above hymn reverberated everywhere. A startled Swayambhu sprang up from his bed; the hymn was still ringing in his mind. He immediately looked for the palm leaf script that had these words written on it. After a bit of frantic searching, he found the leaf that had the exact script and the purpose of the hymn. It was to be recited when a person was about to wear the *Panchamukhi Rudraksh.*

The word Rudraksh literally means the 'Tear drops of Shiva'. Rudraksha were joint together to make a garland and used as prayer beads by the devotees of Lord Shiva. Panchamukhi translated to Five Faces. The five faces represented the *pancha bootha, five primordial elements. Akasha, Vayu, Agni, Aapaha and Prithvi* - Space, Wind, Fire, Water and Earth.

Swayambhu was now in a state of trance, he knew his calling had been answered by Mahadev. He found the vehicle that would be the transporter of the aggregated energy. It would be a *Panchamukhi Rudraksh*. The human body was made of the *pancha bootha,* and the most revered tree was the Rudraksha tree from which the *Panchamukhi Rudraksh* originated. Swayambhu closed his eyes and recited 'Om *Namah Shivaya.'*

A few days later, there was a meeting organized in Velliangiri. A day that would define a new dawn, not just for the Gunas and Suras but probably for the rest of the southern peninsula. All the stakeholders were assembled in the royal meeting chamber of Swayambhu. He was seated on his throne with Shakthi by his side. Rishabha, Vignesh, Prajapathi, Deva, Prajwal, Pawan, and Chandra were the other attendees. Chandra had been briefed by Swayambhu and Shakthi privately, and he felt absolutely blessed to be part of this divine intervention.

Swayambhu began to address the audience:

'You are all aware that I firmly believe nature always finds a way to balance through procreation and destruction in equal measure so that the balance is maintained all the time. *prakruthi, nature* is a manifestation of the divine and it is the will of the divine to bring about any change.

'Lord Mahadev has his own plans and we are mere instruments in the game of life. The recent series of events, undoubtedly guided by the divine, have led us to this moment and I have simply submitted to his will.'

Swayambhu delved on the sequence of events that would need to take place for the birth of the warrior. He would do a penance to aggregate his *Kundalini Shakthi* and create the epicentre. The primordial energy would be transferred to a *Panchamukhi Rudaraksh*. It would be carried by Prajwal to the sacred river Vaiyai, where it would be consecrated. Once the consecration is completed, it would be handed over to Krithika. Krithika would need to wear the Rudraksh around her neck and perform a penance to Lord Mahadev for six days for the energy to be transferred from the Rudraksha to her body.

'The only remaining piece of the puzzle is to get a scared Panchamukhi,' said Swayambhu.

The *Panchamukhi Rudraksh* was found in the faraway land of Nepal, close to Mount Kailash.

'I am hoping that Mahadev shows us the way for this too,' said Swayambhu.

Just as Swayambhu finished this sentence, one of the soldiers came into the room and whispered something in the ear of Rishabha.

'What is it, Rishabha?' asked Swayambhu noticing the interruption.

Rishabha got up, folded his hands in a Namaste.

'My Lord, there is a *siddhar, enlightened one,* waiting outside to see you. He has come from Agasthyakoodam.

'He wants to hand over something important to you in person that he received on his visit to Pashupathi Nath temple as part of his pilgrimage.'

Swayambhu was overwhelmed with the events that were unfolding.

'Rishabha, bring the *siddhar* in with honours. It is our blessing that he is here,' said Swayambhu.

The *siddhar* walked in, a diminutive figure. Swayambhu felt that he was seeing sage *Agasthya* himself, believed to be the first *siddhar*. Shakthi and Swayambhu knelt down and touched his feet as a mark of respect.

'*Hey rajan, oh king.* During my annual pilgrimage to Kailasam, one day while in Yoga Nidra, I heard a voice in my head that directed me to go to the Pashupathi Nath temple and bring a *Panchamukhi Rudraksh*. I also had a vision of Velliangiri. I felt it was the voice of Lord Mahadev himself, so here I am and here is the *Panchamukhi Rudraksh*,' said the *siddhar.*

The *siddhar* handed over the Rudraksh to Swayambhu and recited **"Om Hreem Kleem Namaha"**

Swayambhu knelt down and touched the feet of the Siddhar once again.

'Mahadev has sent you to help us succeed in our mission.'

'*Har Har Mahadev*!' bellowed Swayambhu.

'*Har Har Mahadev*!' repeated everyone in unison and the sound was so overpowering that it echoed across the halls of the Velliangiri Palace.

BIRTH OF THE WARRIOR

Swayambhu had been closeted in his room for a few days now. Initially, he was in a state of transcendental meditation praying to Mahadev to help him achieve the task. After a few days, he started invoking each of the *pancha bhoothas*, so he could transfer their respective energies into each face of the Rudaraksh. Ordinary mortals have a portion of the *pancha bootha* energy in them and they leave it behind with the primordial elements, when their time comes to leave the earth.

Swayambhu, being a yogi, had higher levels of the *pancha bhootha* energy in him. He used this elevated energy level and transferred it to the Rudraksh. This would enable Krithika to beget an unmatched being who would stand for knowledge, righteousness and courage.

The five faces of the Rudraksh now had the energy of the *pancha bhoothas* in them. It was now time for Swayambhu to build his own internal energy levels to culminate in the *Ajna*. He was a practicing yogi; hence it didn't take tremendous effort for him to awaken his *chakras*.

Swayambhu felt a huge throbbing in the centre of his forehead, he knew it was time!

He took the Rudraksh and placed it in the middle of his forehead, between his two eyebrows, reciting

'Om Nama Shivaya' five times. In ancient times it was believed that Mahadev was represented by *Panchakshara, five syllables* - Na, Ma, Si, Va, Ya. Every primordial element was considered his manifestation as he was the Supreme Lord.

Swayambhu was now in a state of trance for a few minutes, and then he opened his eyes. He looked at the box made of palm leaf next to him. Shakthi had created this box after praying to Mahadev. She had put *vibuthi, sacred ash* in it and kept it under the idol of Mahadev, before leaving it in Swayambhu's chamber as her contribution for the divine task ordered by the Supreme Lord.

Prajwal and Pawan, had been waiting patiently for several days and had maintained chastity and piety because of the divine task they were about to undertake. The door opened and out came Swayambhu with his hair dishevelled and his forehead smeared with *vibuthi*, it felt like Mahadev had come down to earth.

Prajwal and Pawan did a *shashtang namaskaram*. They prostrated full length and touched Swayambhu's feet. '*Chiranjeevi Bhava*,' said Swayambhu and handed over the sacred box to Prajwal, blessing them with immortality.

'May the force be with you.' '*Har Har Mahadev*,' said Swayambhu.

Prajwal and Pawan both repeated in unison in a thunderous voice, before leaving the Velliangiri Palace. Deva and Prajapathi were waiting at the entrance along with Shakthi, Rishabha and Vignesh. All of them touched the box in reverence. The friends mounted their horses and sped away. It was a fairly long journey from Velliangiri to the sacred river of all the clans, Vaiyai.

With prayer on their lips, the two rode in tandem like brothers in arms, through mountains and forests breathing the freshness of the earth.

Swayambhu had warned that the Rudraksh would start generating tremendous amount of heat as they kept riding away from Velliangiri. Pawan was a devoted worshipper of *Vayu, the wind god;* he kept reciting the hymn *"Om Jagathpranaya Vidmahe Dhwaja Hastaya Dimahi Tanno Vayuh Prajothayath".* As they kept riding, there was a consistent cross wind blowing from their left to the right encircling the bag that Prajwal was carrying, as if to keep it cool all the time.

The name Vaiyai was formed from two Sangam Tamil words *Vai* meaning the Earth and *Yai* meaning the Sky. It was believed that the river came from the sky to the earth and hence was associated with divinity and revered by all the clans.

After hours of riding through mountains and plains the duo reached the sacred city of Koodal. Once at Koodal they went to the Devi Temple to pay their obeisance. Here was a goddess whom every clan worshipped. The Goddess had three breasts. It is believed that she was the Goddess of Fertility. Anyone who passed through Koodal always stopped to pay their respects to Goddess *Ayonija*, the one who is self-manifested.

After spending time at the temple, Prajwal and Pawan, started the second part of their journey to the river Vaiyai. They walked for the next couple of days to reach the banks of the Vaiyai River. Even the sand banks of the river were considered holy and could not be trampled with footwear. Once at the river bank, Prajwal and Pawan took the sacred water in their palms and sprinkled it on their head. All rivers were like mothers to the clans.

As Prajwal opened the palm leaf box, there was lightning and thunder above, and it started pouring heavily. The Rudraksh was being cooled both by the river and *Varuna, the god of rain*. Prajwal dipped the Rudraksh in the Vaiyai three times and then with all humility placed it back in its rightful place.

Both the friends went back to the temple ate the *prasad*am, food that was sanctified by offering to the goddess. They slept overnight in the *mandapam, the temple porch*. They got up early morning went to the Vaiyai river for their bath, performed their daily rituals with water and did their *Surya Namaskaram,* a traditional prayer to the Sun God. After finishing their daily routine, they came back to seek the blessings of Goddess Ayonija for the successful completion of their task.

With renewed vigour the two comrades rode to their final destination which was Poigai. The area got its name because of the pond nearby. Krithika lived there. It would take them a few hours to reach Poigai from Koodal. The area was surrounded by hills and forest land; It was a land filled with mist and mystique. As they rode through, they were mesmerized by the pristineness of the region and felt divinity in them.

'Prajwal, I feel purity in every leaf around here,' said Pawan. Prajwal nodded in agreement.

It was late afternoon when they reached the house of Chandra and Krithika. The lordships for the region were awaiting the arrival of Pawan and Prajwal with bated breath. Chandra wore a white *veshti & angavastram,* a tradition long wrap-around and stole worn by the clans. Krithika was wearing a simple *nesavu pudavai,* a woven saree. Both their foreheads were smeared with the Sacred Ash.

The time had come, to pass on the sacred Rudraksh to its rightful owner, Prajwal recited '*Om Namah Shivaya*' thrice and handed over the palm leaf box to Krithika. She looked at with reverence and brought it to her forehead as a mark of respect. She passed it to Chandra, who did the same.

This was a land that prided itself on *virunthombal, hospitality* to guests and treating them as God. After washing their feet outside, Prajwal and Pawan were taken into the Chandra household. In these parts, a very common dish that was served was *kootanchoru, rice mixed with different vegetables* to bring a unique flavour to it. It was followed by *panchamritam* as dessert to mark the special occasion.

After the feast, Prajwal and Pawan rested for the night. Rising early the next morning, they bid goodbye to their great hosts and rode back to Velliangiri. They had completed the divine mission successfully.

It was Friday Morning. Krithika got up early, went for a bath in the Poigai next to her home and prayed to Lord Shiva. The palm leaf box had been kept under the Shiva idol in their *poojai arai, the prayer room.* She took a thread and smeared turmeric on it. It was a custom that a thread dipped in turmeric would become purified with the blessings of Goddess Parvathi. She took the Rudraksh in her hand and placed it on both the eyelids one after the other. She then passed the turmeric thread inside the Rudraksh and made a necklace with the Rudraksh as the Pendant.

She recited **"Om Hreem Kleem Namaha"** 108 times and then wore the Rudraksh. Chandra helped tie the knot behind her neck replicating the procedure of tying the *mangal sutra, sacred thread* used in marriage. After this ritual, for seven days, Krithika maintained celibacy and prayed to Lord Shiva in a small hut built next to the Poigai pond.

After seven days of chanting '*Om Nama Shivaya*', there was a blinding light that emerged from the Rudraksh that Krithika was wearing, she couldn't see a thing as the light engulfed her entire body, she could feel a strong current flowing through her from head to toe.

She kept praying to Lord Shiva and then she fell down unconscious. Krithika was brought back home. She remained at rest for a couple of weeks. Things were normal for some time, but after a couple of months, Krithika fainted again. The *vaithyar, doctor* was called in to check on her; The doctor did *naadi parikshai, a diagnosis through the pulse,* and said she was going to be blessed with a child soon; Chandra was overjoyed. They had wealth, respect and honour. The only thing, missing in their lives was the happiness of a child. He ordered his courtiers to distribute gold coins and food to the entire community. This was a day to remember.

Soon enough, Krithika delivered a baby boy. The boy was so beautiful, no one had seen such a handsome child anywhere in the kingdom. He had sweetness in his smile and sharpness in his eyes. The Supreme Lord had answered the prayers of the Suras. The warrior was born. Word spread about the divine child. News had reached Velliangiri, Swarga and Sathya.

It had been a week since the child was born and a stream of visitors came to Krithika's house to have a glimpse of the baby. It was now time for the boy's naming ceremony. Prajapathi, being the learned Brahman and chief priest was given the task to choose the name for the child.

'Astrology had pointed out that he would be a great warrior born through Swayambhu; he shall hence be called *Muruga, The God of War*,' said Prajapathi. The name brought smiles and joy to all those present in the household. The name itself sounded blissful.

'He is a culmination of the *pancha bootha* and Swayambhu's energies; he shall also be called *Arumugam, the one with* six *facets*,' said Prajapathi. The name sounded as sweet as the boy.

He had come to relieve the Suras from their sufferings, so all the Suras present there prayed to the little boy in silence. Arumuga, end our sufferings.

One of the Suras who was overwhelmed shouted, '*Aro Hara*' in ancient Sangam Tamil language which meant end our sufferings.

'*Muruganukku Aro Hara*', '*Arumuganukku Aro Hara*,' *thundered Deva.*

The entire region was reverberating with the sound of '*Aro Hara.*'

MUSINGS OF MURUGA

Little Muruga was growing up fast. He was the darling of the people in and around Poigai. One evening, Krithika and Maragathavalli were watching the boy's play. Maragathavalli was her *uyir thozhi, soulmate.* During Krithika's penance, Maragathavalli was a pillar of support, taking care of all her needs. Krithika had blessed her, promising that she too would have a child, and their children would become best friends. Muruga was playing with Senguntha, a mighty boy with strong arms, and the son of Maragathavalli. Muruga and Senguntha were close buddies. Maragathavalli had told Senguntha that he must always serve Muruga, as he was a divine child.

It was twilight near Poigai. Krithika waved to Muruga and called him over as it was time to go home. Even as a child, Muruga asked many questions that were beyond Krithika's comprehension. After lighting the *agal,* a *mud lamp,* late in the evening, Krithika instructed Muruga to pray to Lord Shiva in the prayer room. As Muruga closed his eyes and started reciting the *paadal,* hymns in praise of Lord Shiva, Krithika gestured to Chandra with her eyes and asked him to come to the other room.

'*Natha,* the time has come,' said Krithika. She had been telling Chandra that Muruga belonged in Velliangiri, which was his rightful place and not in Poigai. He needed to learn the nuances of the scriptures that Swayambhu could impart to him.

'Kannan was moved to Gokul for a reason but eventually went back to Mathura to achieve his purpose,' said Krithika, quoting the example of Lord Krishna. She felt Muruga was destined for larger things in life beyond his playful childhood.

'*Avan illaamal...*,' Chandra didn't complete his sentence, but Krithika understood his question. Would she be able to live without her child? As a mother, she couldn't, but as a yogini, she knew that a bigger purpose awaited her child.

'Wherever he goes and whatever fame he achieves, he will always be remembered as my child, *Karthikeyan*,' said Krithika, referring to Muruga by his other name. Chandra knew that Krithika had made up her mind and there was no going back. He told Krithika that they would leave tomorrow for Velliangiri.

The next morning, Krithika got up early, started packing little Muruga's belongings, and got him ready for the journey as well.

'*Amma,* where are we going?' asked Muruga inquisitively.

'To your *gurukulam, a residential school.* You will be able to enhance your knowledge there and bring name and fame to our land,' replied Krithika.

'You mean I am going to Velliangiri?' said Muruga. A speechless Krithika knew that the boy had wisdom far beyond his age. She nodded her head in the affirmative.

'*Amma*, I will leave on one condition: that Senguntha also joins me,' said Muruga.

'Of course,' said a voice from behind. Senguntha stood there with a beaming smile along with Maragathavalli.

'Wherever you go, I shall follow you,' and he knelt down, putting his mighty arms in front as a kind of salute to Muruga. Muruga lifted him up and hugged him.

As they loaded the caravan with the items, Muruga stepped out of the house, and a set of peacocks encircled him. He had cared for them and regularly fed them with grains. They had grown extremely friendly and didn't want him to leave. He asked his mother to get the grain bowl, fed each peacock, and held his hands in a *namaskaram* posture, the birds made way for him.

Krithika and party reached Velliangiri the next day. Shakthi was pleasantly surprised to see her half-sister and her beloved son. When Muruga smiled at her, she felt she had seen six smiling faces instead of one. Taken aback, she rubbed her eyes and looked at him again; there was only one little boy. It was just her illusion. Shakthi held out her hand, and Muruga turned back to Krithika, who nodded her head to indicate he should go, he ran to Shakthi who clasped him with both her hands planting a sweet kiss on his cheek.

'You are my little *skanda*,' said Shakthi.

She had seen six faces instead of one but they were all enveloped into one body, and hence she chose to give him the name Skanda.

Swayambhu stepped out from the palace on hearing the commotion outside. As soon as little Muruga saw him, he knelt before him. Swayambhu lifted him and said '*En kannin maniye*,' which meant *apple of my eye*. Krithika then bowed down to Swayambhu along with Chandra.

Holding Shakthi's hand, Krithika said, 'My role is done, dear sister. I have brought him back to the place where he belongs.'

'Muruga's knowledge is way ahead of his time. We felt his next level of learning would be best achieved under the tutelage of Swayambhu,' said Chandra.

Krithika introduced Senguntha to Swayambhu and Shakthi and asked them to take him under their wings as well. The boy prostrated in front of them, and both of them blessed Senguntha and instructed him to stay with Muruga through thick and thin.

After spending the rest of the day with her sister, Krithika and Chandra left for Poigai the next day after bidding farewell to their son.

Muruga started learning ancient scriptures from Swayambhu in right earnest. He would always complete the explanation that Swayambhu started on any scripture, which would bring out a smile on his Guru. Swayambhu swelled with pride at his own creation.

Muruga was becoming the cynosure of everyone's eyes. He was a bundle of playfulness, knowledge, and courage all rolled into one. Shakthi began giving him lessons on warfare and the use of weapons. He also developed great knowledge of Sangam Tamil language and became well- versed in it.

Once, Moothaati, a well-known poet in these parts, was resting under a *mandapam*, a resting place meant for travellers. She saw a cowherd walking towards her. The cowherd told her that she looked tired and weary from her travels, insisting on feeding her tasty blackberries from the tree nearby. Moothaati refused initially, but on the persistence of the cowherd, she accepted to eat the berries. The cowherd then asked her, whether she wanted hot ones or cold ones. Moothaati laughed at the silly cowherd and told him there was no such thing as hot berries. She, however asked him to provide cold berries considering her age. The cowherd hooked his stick and shook the tree vigorously; fruits rolled down and fell on the sand. Moothaati took the fruit and started blowing away the sand. The cowherd immediately asked her, if the berries were hot. A stunned Moothaati knew this was no ordinary cowherd.

'Who are you?' asked Moothaati. The cowherd smiled and replied, 'I am Muruga, son of Swayambhu.' Moothaati folded her hands in a namaskaram and said, '*needuzhi vaazhga*,' blessing Muruga with long life. Muruga returned her salutations by bowing down to the old woman.

'I have heard so much about you. I wanted to play with you and hear you sing the beautiful verses you have composed in Sangam Tamil,' said Muruga.

'I am blessed,' said Moothaati and she sang one in praise of Muruga himself.

In another incident, Rishiraja, a well-known saint had come to Velliangiri. He met Swayambhu and offered him a *kani, a ripe fruit*. It was a prasadam from a special prayer conducted for Lord Vasudeva, considered the protector of the universe. Swayambhu was pleased; he gave it to Shakthi and asked her to divide it into two halves and give it to Vignesh and Muruga as they were the future. Rishiraja intervened and told them that the blessings would be lost if the *kani* was broken; it had to be consumed whole only by one person. Rishiraja left Velliangiri after blessing the couple and their children. Swayambhu was left with a problem to solve.

'I have a test for both of you. Whoever goes around the Velliangiri mountain thrice and returns first will get the *kani*,' said Swayambhu.

Muruga, the one for adventure, immediately ran out and jumped onto a horse gifted to him by his trainer Pawan. The horses travelled like the wind, and Muruga began circumambulating Velliangiri. Vignesh, meanwhile, told his parents, that they were the guardians of all the clans and the flora and fauna of the land. Hence going around them would be equivalent to going around Velliangiri.

Swayambhu and Shakthi could not fault his logic. Vignesh went around his parents thrice and took the *kani*. Muruga landed just then and saw the fruit had been given to his brother.

'You are supposed to uphold the law, and you have cheated me,' said an enraged Muruga pointing his hands towards Swayambhu and left in a huff.

Swayambhu, Shakthi, Ganesh and Rishabha started searching all over for him, but he wasn't to be found. The next day Shakthi received a note from Krithika that a child monk had been spotted in Palani hills, and he resembled Muruga. The entire family took a chariot driven by Rishabha and reached Palani hills. They tried to reason with Muruga to come back. He was not willing to listen to anyone, not even Krithika. Just then, Moothaati came up the hill as she had also heard about the child monk. She told Muruga, that he had taught her to remain humble, and as an elder, it was her turn to teach him.

Moothaati advised Muruga that as a knowledgeable child, he should know that in a family, sacrificing something for a family member's happiness is the greatest contribution one could make. She explained it further by giving the example of Rama, who sacrificed his throne for the sake of his brother. Vignesh, who was standing nearby gave the *kani* to Muruga. Moothaati told Muruga that there were bigger *kani's* waiting for him in his life. Muruga realized his folly and atoned for his anger, returning with his parents to Velliangiri.

A couple of years had passed, Muruga was a young man now. He had by now established his own small fort called Skandha Kottai. Muruga started living there with Senguntha and also his peacock friends. One day, Prajapathi, considered the Guru for the clan, was returning home after visiting Swayambhu and met Muruga in the courtyard, who bowed in front of Prajapathi, but lost in his own thoughts, he didn't reciprocate Muruga's greetings, which angered Muruga.

'Prajapathi,' screamed Muruga. A bewildered Prajapathi turned around to see who was calling out to him.

'Muruga, it's you. I am elder to you; you should not call me by my name,' said Prajapathi.

'Can you please tell me one reason why I should respect you?' asked Muruga, a challenging tone in his voice.

'I am the *Rajaguru, the royal priest,*' said Prajapathi haughtily.

'So, you know the meaning of all mantras, do you?' asked Muruga.

'Of course, I do,' said Prajapathi with a smirk.

'Ok, can you please explain to me the meaning of the word OM?' asked Muruga.

Prajapathi was stumped. It took years of penance and studies to understand the true greatness of the primordial OM. How would he explain it to a young man.

'Muruga, it takes years of training to master it,' said Prajapathi.

'It means you don't know the meaning,' said Muruga, and laughed heartily.

Muruga went on explain the meaning to a stunned Prajapathi.

'You have failed in your duty as a Rajaguru, so I am going to put you under house arrest,' said Muruga and took him to Skandha Kottai.

Deva got to know of this and ran to Swayambhu to free Prajapathi. Swayambhu reached Skandha Kottai and asked Muruga to release Prajapathi as he was the most respected Brahman. Muruga obliged and released Prajapathi.

'Muruga, if you are so knowledgeable, explain the meaning of OM to me,' said Swayambhu.

Muruga pointed out that the Guru was the preacher and the student was the seeker. As was the custom then, Swayambhu would have to bow down and seek the answer from his Guru. Swayambhu agreed and knelt down on one leg in front of Muruga, who explained the meaning of *pranavam*, the primordial sound.

'Today, you have become the teacher to our Lord; hence, you shall be known as Swaminathan,' said Prajapathi.

'You are now a giver of knowledge rather than a seeker; you shall be called *Gnanapanditha*,' said Swayambhu, referring to Muruga as The Master of Knowledge. The transformation of a playful child to The Master was now complete.

DELUSIONAL DEVA

Deva was consumed by thoughts of his former lifestyle and power. He grew restless about reclaiming his kingdom and rescuing his son from the Asuras. Perhaps it was the position that corrupted one's mind. Although he had experienced the supreme intelligence of Muruga through his deeds, he remained unconvinced that this young boy would solve his problems and restore their lost glory. It was also believed in those days that a man with a lot of wisdom would not go to War.

While the entire Velliangiri was abuzz with Muruga's accomplishments, here was Deva, a leader immersed in his own delusions, believing that things had not gone according to plan.

He sent a pigeon courier to his trusted lietenents for a meeting in his palace. Prajwal, Pawan, and Varun duly arrived at Swarga. Deva was pleased to see them.

Dear comrades, 'I think Swayambhu did what he could, but I am not entirely convinced that this young boy is going to solve our problems,' said Deva. 'I see a *pandit* in him rather than a Panther,' he added, pointing out metaphorically that Muruga seemed a wise man, not a warrior.

The three of them were stunned by these remarks. With folded hands, Prajwal said, 'I am the carrier of the Rudraksh. Having witnessed its power up close, I am certain that Muruga will eventually become the warrior you wish to see.'

Pawan added, 'if he possesses knowledge surpassing even Prajapathi, imagine his tactical prowess in a war.'

Varun chimed in, 'O Deva, seasons change with time; there will be rain followed by shine. We can't expect to have rains in summer and monsoon in winter. Patience pays!'

Dear Comrades, 'when we cook rice, our women folk take a morsel of rice and check if it's cooked while it is still on the fire, I think it is time to test Muruga as a warrior,' said Deva. The other three looked at each other.

Prajwal objected vehemently and said 'You want to test Swayambhu's son? Are you serious? we could end up waging a war with Swayambhu himself, and that's a death warrant.'

'All of you are unnecessarily getting worked up. Let's test him. If he fails, then my presumption will be ratified. If he passes the test, we could go and tell Swayambhu that Muruga is ready, and we should sound out the war bugle,' said Deva with a smirk, very proud of his plan.

The orders of the *Sura Pathi, head of the Suras* had to be followed. Even if they didn't agree with his plan, the principles of the clan, ensured that everyone submitted to the will of its leader.

Prajwal sighed and said, 'if we indeed must test him, let's make it a small one, he is just a young man.'

Prajwal suggested testing Muruga's strength by sending his pet Ram, Mesha, a powerful animal, to cause havoc at Skandha Kottai. All of them agreed that was a fair test of Muruga's strength.

Early the next morning, before daybreak, Prajwal left the battering ram at the outskirts of Skandha Kottai and ordered it to show its strength. Mesha ran helter-skelter, breaking down shrubs and small trees. It smashed windows around the fort and unleashed terror among the boys playing there.

Muruga asked Senguntha to check what the commotion was all about. He saw a Ram causing havoc. Senguntha started chasing it. After a pretty long chase, the Ram suddenly stopped and turned around, it went straight for Senguntha' s stomach. Just as it was about to gore him,

Senguntha swiftly moved to his left and caught the horns of Mesha. During the struggle, Senguntha twisted its neck. Mesha was now writhing in pain, and he calmed down. Senguntha tied him with a rope and dragged him along till he reached Muruga.

Mesha, upon seeing Muruga remained motionless, as if it was hypnotized by him. Prajwal, who was waiting on the outskirts of Skandha Kottai couldn't believe his eyes. Muruga was sitting on top of Mesha and riding it out. Prajwal fled from the scene on his horse before he could be spotted.

On reaching Swarga, he ran into the palace to see Deva. He was breathless when he reached the courtroom.

'What news do you bring to me, dear Prajwal?' asked Deva.

'O Deva! Mesha has become like a toy in the hands of Muruga. Senguntha brought him down in one move. I have never seen such powerful boys before, even our soldiers don't dare to go near Mesha,' said Prajwal. 'Muruga has not just passed your test; he will probably come after us now.'

Deva was livid. He gave a stare to Prajwal. 'You are a warrior; you don't run away from the battlefield. Mesha is your belonging. Fight to take him back. Go and avenge Mesha's defeat, that's your duty too,' yelled Deva.

'But Deva...,' said Prajwal,

'Prajwal, it's your right. Even if it is Lord Swayambhu's son. Go now!' said Deva.

Prajwal rode back to Skandha Kottai. As he entered the gateway to Skandha Kottai, he started calling out 'Mesha! Mesha!'

'Who are you and what do you need?' asked Senguntha.

'I am looking for my pet Ram,' replied Prajwal.

'Your pet has caused a lot of damage. You will need to pay a fine to take him back,' said Senguntha sternly.

An enraged Prajwal retorted, 'Young man, do you know who I am? You have such impudence to speak to me in such a manner. Release him, before I do anything untoward.'

Senguntha burst into laughter and said, 'The older goat has come to get its kid.'

Prajwal had heard enough, he swiftly took out his pickaxe, tied to his back and hurled it at Senguntha, just as it was about to hit him, a hand caught the axe in the nick of time.

'Step aside,' said Muruga to Senguntha.

'Being a Sura, you should be fighting the Asuras, not picking petty fights with young boys,' said Muruga and threw the axe back to Prajwal.

'Muruga, don't take advantage of the fact that you are Swayambhu's son,' warned Prajwal.

'Did I!', replied Muruga with a smirk.

'If you think you are that good, I call upon you to fight me,' said Prajwal in a condescending tone.

'Invitation Accepted,' said Muruga gleefully.

Prajwal charged towards Muruga with great fury, holding his axe, he was met with a strong spear, and there was a deafening sound resembling thunder when the two weapons met.

Prajwal raised his axe again, to attack Muruga, this time Muruga bent down swiftly and in a single move tipped the axe with the back of his spear, at the same time sliding and tripping Prajwal down. He then swirled his spear and placed it at the throat of Prajwal, who was on the floor.

'Senguntha, tie him up. Looks like we have a long day ahead,' said Muruga.

Deva got worried now, since Prajwal hadn't returned for quite some time. He sent word for Pawan and asked him to go in search of Prajwal. Pawan reached Skandha Kottai, and saw that Prajwal was tied in the courtyard.

'Muruga, where are you? Release Prajwal immediately,' shouted Pawan, as he rode into Skandha Kottai like a whirlwind.

Muruga stepped out with a smile. He was patience personified.

'Your friend lost to me in battle and hence he is my prisoner. You will have to fight me, if you want to take back your long-lost friend.'

'You are Swayambhu's son, i don't want to hurt you, just release him and I'll spare you,' said Pawan in a stern voice.

'Rules of war don't change, my friend,' said Muruga calmly.

'Well, then prepare to face my wrath,' said Pawan.

Dismounting from his horse, he started swirling the *gada, his mace* to his right and to his left. It created a howling sound as if the cyclone was around the corner.

With a sudden burst of speed, Muruga hurled his spear towards the right hand of Pawan which made the mace fly in the air, and fall quite a distance from him. As a stunned Pawan looked on, Muruga made a leap and landed his feet on Pawan's chest, Muruga raised is hands, and on cue a spear landed in his hand. Senguntha had thrown the spear from behind.

'Looks like we need a bigger stable,' said Muruga with a wry smile.

Deva was done waiting, his anger got the better of him, he summoned his *muhoth, elephant keeper,* to get Airavatha. He climbed on the white elephant, a very rare breed in those times. He tied a quiver full of arrows to his back, held his bow upright, and proceeded towards Skandha Kottai in rage. Airavatha went full throttle, crushing through shrubs, trees and anything that was in its path.

'Muruga come out!' yelled Deva. 'Your impudence has reached unbearable proportions. First you take Prajapathi as a prisoner, and now Prajwal and Pawan. You are the Lord's son. Such behaviour is unbecoming of a prince.'

'Greetings, Sura Pathi! Is it right on your part to test the courage and ability of his Lordship's son?' said Muruga nonchalantly.

Deva knew his game was up, but his pride wouldn't accept defeat.

'Muruga, I challenge you to a battle with me,' said Deva. 'Sure, if you insist, Sura Pathi,' said Muruga gleefully.

Deva strung multiple arrows from the quiver to his bow and took aim. Muruga closed his eyes for a few seconds, and three peacocks arrived near him. Muruga mounted on them, and they flew up, bringing him to the same level as Deva. A stunned Deva was about to release the arrows, when Muruga hurled his spear, which broke Deva's bow in two. It was as if *vajra, lightning bolt,* had struck Deva. Muruga jumped from the peacocks and landed on Airavatha. He whispered something into its ear. Suddenly the elephant folded its legs and sat down. It jolted Deva, who fell down from his seat as Airavatha sat down. Muruga had learnt a thing or two about elephants from his elder brother Vignesh. As Airavatha sat down, Muruga slid down its trunk and reached the ground. Swiftly picking up his spear, he swirled it and placed it in front of Deva's neck.

Deva became a captive too. All the key personnel from the Sura clan were now prisoners of war under Muruga.

The next day, news reached Prajapathi. He went to Velliangiri and briefed Swayambhu. Prajapathi and Swayambhu arrived at Skandha Kottai.

'O Muruga, you are a *brhama gnani, all knowing.* When man is in a state of insecurity, he can't differentiate between a rope and a snake. He also doesn't know whom to trust and whom not to. His actions are driven by fear which is another form of anger. Please pardon the Suras and release them,' said Prajapathi and joined his hands in a *namaskaram* position.

Muruga smiled and asked Senguntha to release the three Suras. All of them sought Muruga's pardon.

'O Deva, when you ask the Lordship for help and he has obliged, have the patience and forbearance to let the process take its prescribed path and reach its logical end.'

'*Yam Irukka Bayamen*,' said Muruga, raising his hands in a blessing position. The words were from Sangam Tamil, which meant, *why fear when I am here*.

'Aro Hara! Aro Hara! Aro Hara!' reverberated all across Skandha Kottai.

THE ANOINTED ONE

A few years had passed since the skirmishes involving Deva and Muruga. Muruga had now reached *yavvanam,* exuding confidence and reflecting youthful vitality.

On a bright sunny day at Velliangiri, Swayambhu received visitors. Rishabha escorted them to the meeting hall, where Swayambhu and Shakthi welcomed their visitors. It was Deva and his wife, Sachi. If it was a business visit, Deva would have come alone, since they had come as family, they knew it was not a business visit.

Deva and Sachi greeted Swayambhu and Shakthi with their *namaskaram* before taking their seats.

'Lord, I come with two wishes, hoping you would grant them both,' said Deva holding his hands in namaskaram.

'Go Ahead, Deva! I am all ears,' said Swayambhu.

'Muruga has now grown to be a handsome young man. He has the wisdom and courage to lead. I seek your approval and blessings to anoint him as the Commander- in-Chief of the Sura Army,' said a proud Deva.

Acknowledging Muruga's natural prowess as a warrior, Swayambhu readily accepted the proposal, with Shakthi also concurring.

'Thank you, my Lord. The Suras will always be indebted to you and your clan,' said Deva with a beaming smile.

'What is your second wish?' asked Swayambhu with a smirk.

Deva glanced at Sachi and hesitantly brought up the second topic.

'Lord, you know our daughter, Amruthavalli, who has attained marriageable age. Sachi and I felt that there would be no better match for our daughter than Muruga. We would love to have Muruga as our *mappillai, son-in- law.'* Deva paused, and waited with bated breath for Swayambhu's reply.

Shakthi was the first to reply, 'Amrutha has all the *sathgunangal, good virtues* needed for a girl. She will complement Muruga in his journey. I am very happy to have her as my daughter in law.' She then looked towards Swayambhu for his concurrence.

'Let us consult Muruga too, after all, it's his marriage,' said Swayambhu.

Word was sent to Muruga, who arrived at Velliangiri. He was accompanied by his best man, Senguntha. Shakthi was overjoyed on seeing her handsome son. She hugged him tightly with motherly affection, a feeling every mother experiences when seeing her child after a long time. Even when they are grown-ups, they always remain children to their parents.

Muruga was pleased to hear the news of him being chosen as Commander-in-Chief of the Sura Army. He was happy to take Amrutha as his lawful wedded wife, but only after he won the war for the Suras.

As the news spread, the entire Sura clan rejoiced. The time for their redemption had come and soon they would get back their kingdom, Indraprastha. Deva was elated with the developments; this was like getting two mangoes from the tree by throwing one stone.

Deva went to Sathya, the abode of Prajapathi, to get the auspicious dates for Muruga's consecration as the Commander of the Sura Army and for his daughter's engagement and wedding.

As the day of consecration approached, there was palpable tension in the Deva household. The Lord's son and their future son-in-law would be coming to their house to be anointed the Commander of their army. There were *malais and thoranams, garlands and decorations* all across Swarga. This was one-of-a-kind moment, a divine child born for a specific purpose would become their leader and eventually their saviour. Deva left no stone unturned to make the occasion, the most memorable one that had been witnessed in recent times.

On the appointed day, Muruga arrived at Swarga on a horse-driven chariot, driven by Lord Swayambhu himself. Rishabha and Senguntha rode ahead, while Shakthi was in another Chariot along with Chandra, Krithika and Vignesh. Prajapathi had already reached Deva's abode so that the rituals could be performed as per the scriptures.

When Muruga reached the gates of Swarga, Sachi and others performed an *arathi* ritual. The ritual involved making a solution from turmeric on a plate and circling the plate in front of the individual and discarding the solution near the person's feet to ward off evil eyes. Deva garlanded Muruga and escorted him to a specially decorated *simhasanam, throne*. Once Muruga sat on the throne, Vedic chants reverberated from the Deva household. All the guests assembled there threw *akshathai* on Muruga as a mark of blessing for the newly appointed Commander-in-Chief. It consisted of a mix of rice and turmeric considered a symbol of purity and prosperity.

Deva raised his right hand, and there was pin-drop silence around.

Deva sought Swayambhu's approval to speak by bringing his hands together in *namaskaram*. Swayambhu nodded his head in agreement.

'My dear Suras, this is a day of reckoning for us. We have suffered for long, at the hands of the Asuras. Our Kingdom is gone and your prince Jayanthan is captive. Muruga is here now, so fear not. Join hands with him, as we sound the war bugle against the Asuras to reclaim what is ours. We shall win, as we have the blessings of Lord Mahadev, who has sent Muruga to us.'

'On behalf of the entire Sura clan, I pronounce Muruga our *Thalapathi, commander of the army*,' concluded Deva.

'*Thalapathi Vaazhga Vaazhga!* screamed the entire gathering. A phrase used for blessing their commander with long life. It was followed by '*Aro Hara, Aro Hara!*'

As the slogans continuing to pierce the sound barrier, Deva handed over a shining sword to Muruga. It reflected Muruga's handsome face. He accepted it gleefully and put it in its *urai, scabbard.*

Shakthi now stepped forward and presented a *Thanga Vel, a golden spear.* It had the sacred ash smeared on both sides of its face. Muruga took the *Vel* and brought it to his eyes, a mark of respect for the weapon given by Shakthi. Anything given to a child by its mother with love is the greatest blessing that can be received.

Muruga stood with the *Vel* to his side, and the visual was just mesmerizing. It felt like time stood still. The entire Sura clan and other guests were witnessing a handsome warrior, who could just kill with his looks. He now had a powerful weapon too.

'Shakthi Vel Muruganukku Aro Hara!' said Deva and the entire crowd shouted in unison 'Aro Hara, Aro Hara!'

Muruga folded his hands in *namaskaram* and bowed to everyone. Now it was his turn to speak. The entire crowd listened to him in rapt attention.

'Dharma is supreme above all else. I am honoured to be given the opportunity to re-establish dharma and return to you what is rightfully yours. No force will stop me from delivering my promise. I have the blessings of my parents, the best wishes of my brother, and my dearest Senguntha to help me fulfil my promise and I will succeed.'

'I would also like to point out to you that the Sura clan should remain rooted to the ground when you get your kingdom and wealth back. Power and Wealth both corrupt. It is important to balance the material with the spiritual, and that's what our ancestors and our scriptures have taught us. Let us follow it, in both letter and spirit. Believing in the supreme being and following the path of Bhakti is what we all need to do as individuals and I would do everything at my disposal to spread this message far and wide,' concluded Muruga.

Prajapathi, Deva, and Swayambhu felt a sense of pride. Here was a young man, speaking far beyond his age. For Shakthi and Krithika,

Muruga wasn't their little child anymore. He had grown to become a Leader and a Guru, one treated with reverence.

The guests were treated to a sumptuous meal, followed by special drink only available with the Suras: the *Somapanam, elixir of immortality.* It created intoxication for sure, while some believed it also provided immortality.

After the festivities died down, there was another guest at the doorstep of Swarga. It was the well-known sage, Rishiraja. Everyone greeted him with respect and he was offered a seat in the household. Deva felt blessed that a great sage had made a visit at the most opportune time. He blessed Muruga, *'Vijayi Bhava', may you be victorious.* Deva explained the reason for the festivities.

Rishiraja smiled and said 'O Deva, I am aware of your desires and I know Muruga's destiny.'

He called out to Muruga and asked him to sit beside him. Rishiraja wanted to provide Muruga with some insight, before he embarked on his journey.

'Listen to me Muruga,' said Rishiraja and started his diatribe.

'In war it is important to understand your enemy. Be aware of their abilities, their strengths and be well prepared before taking on their might. Most importantly, never underestimate the opponent. I know the path you are planning to take. Let me share a small glimpse of who you are up against and what are his strengths.'

'You are poised to take on Sooran to win back the kingdom of the Suras. Like you have Senguntha as your trusted lieutenant, Sooran has his brother Tharakan, who lives in the town of Mayapuri. A land known for its Wizards and Wizardry. As the name suggest, the town is illusion personified. You would need to successfully defeat Tharakan before reaching Sooran. Even Rama had to overcome Indrajith before reaching Ravana. Your uncle Sundara tried to help Deva by trying to vanquish Tharakan but in vain. May be its your destiny that you will finish the task.

After a pause, Rishiraja continued. 'On the way to Mayapuri, you will encounter *Krauncha Malai, the sea- shell mountain* because of its unique shape. It used to be revered long time ago but has now become a demon's abode. Beware of Banu, Sooran's son. The one who has captured Jayanthan and has him as the prisoner of war. He is a formidable foe. Sooran is the undisputed warlord in all of South India and lives in the city of Mahendrapuri.'

'Oh, dear *Vela*,' he said, referring to Muruga as the one with the spear.

'May the force of Lord Mahadev be with you and let Lord Vishnu protect you,' concluded Rishiraja. He put his hands on Muruga's forehead to bless him and recited loudly,

'Narayana Narayana Narayana!'

WAR GAMES BEGIN

After the festivities had subsided, Swarga became the strategic centre for planning the impending war against the Asuras. Rishiraja had earlier provided the background information and outlined the sequence of events necessary for winning the war. The time had come to gather the army.

Swayambhu gathered the Gana warriors needed to support Muruga in his quest to establish Dharma. Shakthi joined in and devised a war slogan based on the weapon she had bestowed upon her son.

She lifted her hands above her head and sounded the war cry, '*Vetri Vel–Veera Vel!*' the entire gana tribe thundered '*Vetri Vel-Veera Vel!*' Its purpose was to convey to the army that they were behind a courageous leader and a Victory spear.

Away at Swarga, it was Deva's turn, to address the Sura warriors.

'Dear brothers, here is your chance at redemption. You have the greatest warrior that our clans have ever seen, leading this war. You are the shoulders and arms of Muruga, who will carry him back to our land as a victorious commander.'

Deva raised both his hands above his head in a *namaskaram* and shouted '*Aro Hara!*' and the entire Sura battalion reciprocated the war cry, causing the earth beneath them to tremble. The entire Sura army then left for Velliangiri.

Pawan, known for his speed, was chosen as the *sarathy, charioteer* for Muruga. He was more than pleased to have this honour bestowed on him by Swayambhu. Pawan bowed to Swayambhu, went on one knee and extended his right hand, pledging that nothing would happen to Muruga, as long as he remained.

Senguntha selected strong young men from his tribe and trained them in swordsmanship and spear combat. He had also reached out to young men in Poigai, who were willing to participate in a dharmic war led by Muruga. Many decided to pledge their lives for Muruga's sake.

Senguntha had assembled a sizeable army of fearless warriors, lacking experience in warfare but not determination. They were stationed at Skandha Kottai and accompanied Senguntha and Muruga to Velliangiri.

It was now time for the supreme commander to address the battalion. Muruga stood on his chariot to address them.

'You are brave soldiers following the path of Dharma, our scriptures have always taught us that Dharma may be tricked through deceit but dharma will triumph in the end. We are blessed souls to be given this opportunity to make things right.

I am not your commander; I am one of you. We are like the clenched fist, where all the tribes have united for a noble cause. Let us complete our task and return victorious.'

Muruga let out the war cry '*Vetri Vel-Veera Vel!*' and the entire army thundered in unison.

'Senguntha, lead our army to *Krauncha Malai* and establish our position there. Meet Tharakan, and propose a peaceful transfer of power back to the Suras, else warn him that he would have to face war,' said Muruga.

'As you command, my Lord,' said Senguntha.

The huge battalion marched towards *Krauncha Malai*, shaking the earth below with its march.

At a distance in Mayapuri, the court room witnessed a laugh that would make thunder feel ashamed. It was Tharakan, the all-powerful wizard and the right-hand man of Sooran.

'Swayambhu has completely lost his mind. He is sending a boy to fight with us because he has given his word that he wouldn't go to war with us.'

'Ha Ha Ha Ha!' he roared in laughter and continued;

Swayambhu has become senile. Its destiny that his son has to die at my hands.'

Someone from the courtroom interrupted to tell Tharakan that he was no ordinary boy and had taken the main warriors of the Sura clan as captives.

'Ah! Deva and his troops are imbeciles, they wouldn't want to antagonize Swayambhu and would have simply surrendered. They are just playing mind games with us,' concluded Tharakan.

As Senguntha led Muruga's Army to *Krauncha Malai*, they saw that Tharakan was already there with his army, waiting for them. It looked like he had spies all over the land and knew about their arrival beforehand.

'Who are you?' thundered Tharakan to Senguntha.

'Tharaka, I am Muruga's humble servant, here to inform you that Jayanthan should be released and their kingdom and wealth returned to the Suras, else Sooran would have to face Muruga's wrath.'

Tharakan burst out laughing and said, 'You have no idea who you are up against. I will spare your life, just turn around and leave.'

'I am not leaving anywhere, till you are captive,' said Senguntha with a smirk.

Tharakan lifted his bow and started shooting one arrow after the other at Senguntha.

Senguntha was no ordinary warrior, he had learnt the use of the *astras, weapons* from Swayambhu himself. Senguntha broke all the arrows of Tharakan with his counter arrows. Before Tharakan could react, Senguntha fired an arrow that broke Tharakan's crown into pieces. The enraged Tharakan was about to pick another set of arrows from his quiver to fire at his opponent, when Senguntha's arrows brought down his chariot by breaking its wheels. This incensed Tharakan even further; he knew he had to use other means to defeat Senguntha.

He lifted a weapon which was in the shape of a snake and hurled it at Senguntha, who became immobile for a minute but regained his composure soon enough. Meanwhile Tharakan had used the *astra* on the soldiers too, who became immobile. Now Tharakan decided to bring more wizardry into play. He started to appear all across the warzone. Senguntha knew the time had come to use some wizardry himself. He started to replicate Tharakan's tricks, appearing across the warzone. Tharakan knew he had met his match and decided to use trickery. He escaped into the caves of *Krauncha Malai*.

Senguntha chased Tharakan into the cave; there was total darkness. Tharakan had tricked Senguntha into entering the hill, not realizing that Tharakan controlled it with his wizardry. In a rush of adrenaline, Senguntha forgot sage Rishiraja's words. Tharakan had succeeded in bringing Senguntha into the cave like a pitcher plant engulfs its prey. Tharakan created a purple haze which made Senguntha unconscious.

Seeing that their leader did not return, a portion of the army went inside the cave to support their leader; they were engulfed by the purple haze too and fell unconscious. Surprisingly, Tharakan didn't kill them.

He wanted to use them as bait to lure Muruga into the battle. He wanted to triumphantly report to his brother after defeating Muruga.

A soldier was dispatched as a messenger to inform Muruga that Senguntha had been captured and his life was in peril. As always Muruga was thinking ahead, he knew that he was being lured into the battle by Tharakan. Muruga smiled and said 'fear not, I will take on Tharakan and free Senguntha and others.'

Tharakan waited on the battle field, he knew Muruga would arrive.

Muruga swiftly arrived on the battle field aboard a chariot propelled by Pawan, travelling at the speed of wind. Upon seeing Muruga, Tharakan let out a huge roar of laughter.

'Adei,' shouted Tharakan, a term used to belittle someone and continued,

'We don't have any enmity with your father, why have you come here? I also didn't kill your friend for the same reason, but I wanted to teach him a lesson for his impudence, hence I have held him captive.'

At a distance, the Asura army had tied Senguntha and others with a rope to a large tree. They had been released from the spell of the purple haze by Tharakan.

'Take your friends and leave now,' yelled Tharakan.

'Tharaka, I don't have any enmity with you either, but you and your brother have wronged the Suras and my job is to restore Dharma. If you return what you owe them, I am happy to leave.

Adei,' said Tharakan again, raising his voice this time.

'Looks like the Suras have been giving you a lot of somapanam beyond your capacity,' and laughed with disdain.

'Before you take one step further, know that your uncle lost to me in battle and begged for my mercy.'

'Hey Tharaka, I am a warrior by birth. I don't have the habit of going back; I only look at what's in front of me. If you are brave enough, fight me instead of this empty talk,' retorted Muruga nonchalantly.

'Muruga, prepare for your death,' said Tharakan and raised his bow.

Just as he lifted his bow, he saw twelve arrows coming at him simultaneously, striking his crown and the rest of his body, he was completely incapacitated and was bleeding, he had never seen anyone use the bow and arrow like this before.

In sheer desperation, he used his wizardry and caused a massive explosion on *Krauncha Malai*. The hill exploded into pieces, hitting the armies with its might, killing many instantly. He disappeared from Muruga's sight and hid behind one of the huge boulders of rock that had fallen.

It was now or never for Taraka. Behind the rock, Tharakan closed his eyes and started chanting verses of black magic. A discus appeared on his outstretched left hand. Tharakan used his wizardry and black magic to build powers to it. He took it in his hand and started rotating it in his fingers, it was rotating so ferociously in his fingers, that it resembled the *chakra* of Lord Vishnu. Muruga's army was scared to death. They felt their end was near. Everyone started saying their prayers. Tharakan let out a thunderous laughter and threw the *chakra,* which was now rotating furiously, as it sped towards Muruga. Muruga hurled his *Vel* at it, causing sparks to fly as the chakra fell down. Muruga jumped out of his Chariot and ran towards Tharakan, picking up the *Vel* on the ground. Tharakan and the army were stunned by what they had just witnessed. This was no ordinary young man; they believed that Muruga was possibly a manifestation of Lord Shiva himself.

A portion of the *Krauncha Malai* stood between Muruga and Tharakan. Muruga raised his *Vel* and hurled it. It burst through the rock like a sharp knife slices through food and landed on Tharakan's chest, bringing him instant death.

'Vetri Vel-Veera Vel!' reverberated all around the area where *Krauncha Malai* once stood, and the army marched towards the south, rejoicing in the victory of their commander.

Deva and Prajwal, witnessing the battle that took place, came running and fell at the feet of Muruga. Muruga dipped the *Shakthivel* smeared in blood into a bowl of water that he carried from Poigai. He believed it purified the *Vel.*

'Muruga, you have killed one of the most heinous Asuras of our times,' said Deva with a sense of devotion.

'It is a step towards restoring Dharma back. In the future, people should remember what happened in *Krauncha Malai,'* said Prajwal.

'I agree,' said Pawan.

'Muruga, I would like to create a statue of you here, as a symbol of your victory,' said Deva. It could serve as a testament for future generations. They would know that the Dharmic war started here in *Krauncha Malai.*

'Deva, I am not *Sarweshwaran*; I am a human,' said Muruga in a calm manner, referring to another name of Lord Shiva.

'It is my destiny to serve the Suras, establishing righteousness as prescribed in our scriptures. I owe my success so far to the blessings of Lord Mahadev. If we do have to build a statue it should be that of Lord Mahadev, he is the one who destroys the Asura outside and the Asura within us,' concluded Muruga.

'Muruga, your words are all pearls of wisdom, I dare not question. However, I would like to make a suggestion. Since Tharakan was killed by you using the *Shakthi Vel*, we will build a temple of Goddess Parvathi here. For us, Shakthi is like mother Parvathi. We will also have your statue, built in honour of your victory,' concluded Deva.

'Deva, you are a king, I am just your commander. Your wish and the wishes of the Suras and Ganas is my command. I bow to your affection and respect,' said Muruga.

The entire army tossed their weapons into the air as a gesture of jubilation.

Deva sent word to his chief architect to build a temple for Goddess Parvathi. A statue of Muruga was to be made inside the sanctum sanctorum of the temple with the name *Kumara Swamy* inscribed on it, meaning The Lord's son.

SOORAN VOWS REVENGE

Gloom descended on the once-powerful Mayapuri. The king, once considered invincible, was killed. News had reached the *Maharani,* the queen of Mayapuri. A screaming Sowri ran to the outskirts of the city towards her deceased husband. She cradled his lifeless body on her lap and started lamenting the misfortune that had befallen them.

'The Suras were like scared dogs, who would hide their tails between their legs when you approached. How could you have been slain by them? Your majestic presence gave the Asuras dignity and pride. You were the linchpin for Sooran, our king of kings. The days of doom have arrived on our clan,' lamented Sowri.

The other concubines of the king also reached the war zone and started crying inconsolably.

Indiran, the son of Tharakan, heard the news while away from the kingdom and rushed back to Mayapuri. Sowri, seeing her son, was even more inconsolable now. Overcome with emotion, both Sowri and Indiran hugged each other and let out an *olam, a cry of lament.*

'*Amma,* I am a *paavi*,' said Indiran, calling himself a sinner.

'I was not around to fight for my father and our kingdom.'

'I have let him down and our people. I have brought shame upon the Asura clan.'

The time for the last rites had come. As part of the custom in those days, Sowri wished to perform *udan kattai eruthal, joining the funeral pyre* as a form of suicide. Indiran, taken aback by this, pleaded with his mother. He had just lost his father, and his mother wished to die along with his father and be burned alive. Indiran pleaded with his mother.

'This is not the time for you to go, mother. I will be left an orphan. I will avenge father's death.

'Be by my side, be my support, help me get our glory back.'

Sowri looked at her son calmly and said, 'I wish you well, and may you succeed in your mission, but I have decided I will follow our centuries-old tradition.'

Hearing this, the other queens said they would join the ritual as well. Indiran begged and pleaded with his mother, but she remained steadfast in her decision. With a heavy heart, he lit all the pyres and completed the last rites of the entire family.

Watching the burning pyres, Indiran wondered why the country needed such a custom of a woman being burned alive on her husband's funeral pyre. '*Sura or Asura, this system needs to go,*' he said to himself.

Indiran went back to an empty palace in Mayapuri. There was a deafening silence all around; he couldn't bear it and he left immediately for Mahendrapuri.

Indiran entered the courtroom of Mahendrapuri where his *periyappa, his father's elder brother,* was seated. Overcome with emotion, he ran towards him, fell at his feet, and started crying inconsolably.

'Indira,' said Sooran in a booming voice.

'You are not just Indiran, you are Asurendran. Never forget that.'

'Don't be a coward, ever. Face everything with your chest puffed-up and fight it with pride. Stop lamenting and tell me what happened.'

'Asureshwara, I have lost my father. Your brother is no more. Additionally, my mother has also committed suicide by climbing on the funeral pyre as a part of our age-old tradition. I am orphaned,' lamented an inconsolable Indiran.

Sooran laughed with disdain and said, 'Stop day-dreaming and tell me what actually happened. Have you come to my court to tell me speculative news to cause sensation and get noticed?'

'*Periyappa...,*' screamed Indiran.

'I am not a little boy to come to the king of kings and create some sensational news just to get noticed. I have genuinely lost my father; you have lost your right-hand man, your *valathu kai*. The Asura clan has lost one of its greatest warriors.'

He broke down once again, falling at Sooran's feet.

Sooran was simultaneously enraged and sorrowful. He had lost his beloved brother, a pillar of strength to him and an outstanding warrior of his clan. His eyes turned red and tears rolled down his cheeks. The mighty Asura was human after all.

Sooran lifted Indiran up and hugged him tightly, tears flowing down his own cheeks.

Sooran then looked at his face and said, 'My dear nephew, fear not, I am there for you. Now tell me exactly what happened.'

Indiran wiped his tears and said, 'Periyappa, I was not in town when the Suras' attack occurred. I was told the Suras launched an attack unexpectedly along with a young man who was leading their army. I am told his name is Muruga.'

'He has destroyed the *Krauncha Malai* and brought it down to earth. He has also destroyed the *malai* that protected you,' said Indiran, referring to his father as a rock that shielded Sooran.

Sooran was a bundle of emotions and started reminiscing the heydays with his great warrior brother.

'I also understand that they are heading south probably towards Mahendrapuri,' said Indiran.

'Tharaka..., every clan including the Suras trembled when you walked on their land. I can't believe the giant mountain has been brought down. I will miss those arms that used to hug me. Rest in peace, my brother,' said Sooran in anguish. Soon, his anguish turned into anger.

'Deva, you are finished,' he bellowed from the bottom of his stomach.

Sooran clapped his hands, and his bodyguards and commander came and stood before him. He instructed them to ready themselves with the deadliest weapons available.

'Comrades, the time has come for us to finish this war once and for all. We have been winning and losing battles to the Suras; this will be the mother of all battles. We shall remove every Sura from this earth. Join me, as I avenge my brother's death and restore the pride of invincibility to the Asura clan,' thundered Sooran.

'Indira, I will show this boy wonder you are referring to, the might of the Asuras. Not only him, but his entire clan will forever be our slaves,' concluded Sooran.

The look on Sooran's face resembled that of an angry Lord Rudra, the fiercest form of Lord Shiva with his third eye open. His body was trembling with rage. He was like a ferocious beast waiting to devour anything in its path.

When Sooran had finished, there was pin-drop silence in the courtroom. Suddenly, a voice said *manna, dear king*.

Sooran looked around and saw that his minister had stood up with folded hands in *namaskaram*. He was one of the most respected ministers in his cabinet, Amothakan, whose name interestingly meant, one who seconds a proposal of the king.

'Amothaka, you always second my thoughts, I guess you have now stood up to tell me that you accept my call for war.'

'Mannar manna, O king of kings, I agree that you need to avenge your brother's death, if it is indeed true. I am not doubting Indiran's truthfulness, but we need to find out the whole truth. Please don't get agitated with my suggestion. As your interior minister, it is my duty to suggest this,' said Amothakan bowing to his Lordship.

'Amothaka!' shouted Sooran. 'Are you saying, I just sit quietly after listening to my nephew? Is that Kshatriya dharma?'

'My Lord, I understand the pain that Indiran is suffering due to his father's demise. I also understand your emotional turmoil from losing your brother. In situations like these, it's important to pause and think through before taking any decision. Emotional decisions do not always have a positive outcome.'

'Are you suggesting that I wait here for that boy to come along with Deva and his cronies and then fight them in a war? They need to suffer my wrath. I want to destroy them even before they think of coming here,' screamed Sooran.

'My Lord, continued Amothakan, 'We need to ascertain facts from fiction. We need to identify who is this new boy leading the Sura Army. Why are the Suras suddenly gung- ho about fighting a war with us, when they were in hiding and lived like nomads till now? There is more than meets the eye. We need to explore further.'

'Amothaka!' bellowed Sooran again.

'Are you suggesting, that i have to fear a small boy in battle or those incompetent Suras who kept running to Swayambhu or Sundara, time and again, when they were defeated by us. I would rather die in battle rather than beg for help or mercy. Asuras have had the guts to fight anyone without fear. We have learnt this from our ancestors for several eons.'

'My Lord, pardon me if my statement made you feel that way. What has happened to Tharaka cannot be pardoned. We have always believed that another Asura rises from the blood of one. We live and die with that principle. I am all for war, but I just want us to think strategically and be well prepared because of the new boy. If Tharakan had been vanquished by the Suras, I would have been the first to endorse your war cry.'

Sooran started seeing that Amothakan's words made a lot of sense. He sat down on his throne, put his hand on his chin, looked up with his eyebrows raised.

'What do you propose, Amothaka?' said Sooran in a calm demeanour.

'My Lord, we need to ascertain the details of the new warrior. We need to find out if they have better weapons than before. Let us send our messengers and spies out. Indiran had mentioned that they are moving south from *Krauncha Malai*. We know the fastest routes and darker routes to *Krauncha Malai*. Our spies can gather all the information and send it to us via pigeon couriers. We will then ambush them before they realize what hit them.'

'My Lord, continued Amothakan. We will avenge Tharaka's death, you are born to rule, and your might is several times greater than your brother's, and you also have all of us. I am sure that the Suras will not be foolhardy to just land up at Mahendrapuri to fight you.'

'Trust us, my lord; we will ensure the death of the new boy and the Suras. It will be spoken about for generations, as a story of great valour of our Asura Clan,' said Amothakan and sat down.

Sooran was thoroughly convinced by his minister's advice. He clapped his hands and a soldier walked in.

'Get me Pakan, Mylayan, and Seeran,' screamed Sooran referring to his three trusted spies.

After a while, a soldier arrived and informed that the three spies were waiting to meet him. Sooran gestured for them to be brought in.

The three spies folded their hands in namaskaram and bowed before the king.

'I have an important task for you three. We are anticipating a deadly war. Go to *Krauncha Malai* and gather all information you can about a boy warrior, the Suras, their weapons, and who else is with them to support their battle. Leave Now,' commanded Sooran.

'*Mannar manna*, we are at your service. We will gather all possible information to ensure victory for us. It is our privilege to serve you and our clan,' said Pakan. He folded his hands in *namaskaram* and the three spies bowed down to Sooran.

Sooran raised his hands in a gesture to bless them for succeeding in their endeavour, and then waved his right hand, indicating for them to leave.

THE SOUTHERN SOJOURN

Muruga and the entourage were now on their journey down south towards Mahendrapuri. It was a long journey, so they decided to take a few breaks along the way. Muruga was still a young man and was inquisitive to learn a lot about Lord Mahadev.

'Deva, to make the journey interesting, why don't you narrate anecdotes about Lord Mahadev,' said Muruga.

'Muruga, you have had your tutelage under Swayambhu, the most learned and respected man among all the clans. What can I tell you, more than what you would already know,' said Deva humbly, hands held in *namaskaram*.

'Deva, listening to the *ithihasas* and *puranas* that talk about the greatness of Lord Shiva, you learn something new every time. It opens up different perspectives with each narration. It is hence important for us to keep listening to the various anecdotes described in our scriptures over and over again.

Deva was overwhelmed with emotion, listening to Muruga's thoughts and felt that he was blessed in many ways to be with Muruga.

'Muruga, it would be my honour to tell you about Lord Mahadev to the best of my knowledge,' said Deva, and bowed his head with hands in *namaskaram* posture and started his narration.

'Maharishi Bhringi, a staunch devotee of Lord Shiva, refused to bow to Parvathi Devi. Parvathi Devi wanted to ensure that Bringu rishi worshipped her along with Shiva, hence she did a penance in the place called Kedar in North India. Lord Shiva, pleased with her penance, decided to make Parvathi the left part of his body. He gave darshan as Lord *Ardhanareeshwara*, the idol of half-woman and half-man. It is a very revered place of worship even today,' said Deva.

'Deva, it not only taught a lesson for the rishi, but for all mankind. Man and woman together make the whole. All of us have masculine and feminine qualities. Both energies together sustain the human soul.' '*Om Nama Shivaya*,' said Muruga and asked Deva to continue.

Speechless with Muruga's take on the episode, Deva continued after a pause, 'Nandi, born to Maharishi Siladha wanted to be the Lord's vehicle forever and did a penance to become a hill in this birth. Lord Shiva accepted his wish and stood on the top of the hill. The hill is in a place called Srisailam and Lord Shiva is worshipped as Mallikarjuna Swamy.'

'Deva, another of Lord's anecdotes to teach us a lesson. Lord is the supreme and we are always his servants. We will always need his feet on our head to be blessed. In the *Kaliyuga*, *bhakti* or devotion is the only means to get the blessings of the Lord. Nandi Bhagwan is the foremost *bhakta* or devotee of the Lord. This anecdote shows us that anyone praying with purity in his heart and bhakti in his mind will be blessed by the Lord.'

Deva continued, 'When Brahma began his creation, Lord Shiva appeared in the form of a mountain. Unaware of the miracles of the Lord, Brahma started creating mountains of his own and found there was no space left, he then realized that the mountain was a manifestation of Lord Shiva and bowed down to him in forgiveness. Lord Shiva told Brahma that he had assumed the mountain form, for the good of the world. The location is called *Pazhamalai, ancient hill.* Whoever ever prays to the Lord there, would get eternal salvation. Kashi in the North of India is a place, where people go to cleanse their sins. *Pazhamalai* is known as the *Dakshina Kashi* or Southern Kashi.'

'What a symbolic way to represent himself,' said Muruga.

'Lord Shiva and Mount Kailash are inseparable. Eventually all living forms which are a manifestation of the *pancha bootha* have to wither away and the soul goes back to the Lord. Worshipping *Pazhamalai* is in a way worshipping Mt. Kailash,' concluded Muruga.

'Muruga, speaking of *pancha bhootha*, we are closing in on one of the sacred places where Lord Shiva is in a unique form as *Nataraja, King of Dance*. It is believed that Lord Shiva manifests in the form of *Akasham, Ether* in this temple. The place is called *Thillai*. It derives its name because of the mangroves that are surrounding the temple,' said Deva.

'Deva, I have heard a great deal about Nataraja Peruman. I would be happy to share my knowledge with you about Nataraja,' said Muruga.

'Nataraja is in a state of eternal bliss and supreme consciousness. Dance is about constant movement and not remaining static. The world keeps changing, seasons keep changing, our body keeps changing, this cycle of balance and imbalance is *prakruthi* and *vikruthi*. The circle around Nataraja represents the Cosmos and the dance of Nataraja is the Cosmic Dance. He is dancing and at the same time remaining still in a state of super consciousness. Each prop and hand gestures have a deeper meaning too.'

'The *udukkai, drum* on the right hand symbolizes creation. *Neruppu, fire* on the left hand denotes destruction. The front hand has the *abhaya muddirai, symbol of protection* and his left hand is in a state of *valampuri or* right warped. It is similar to Lord Ganesha's trunk symbolizing success and prosperity. The left leg is lifted to show grace, at the same time the fingers of the left-hand point towards the left leg, indicating that those who seek solace in him will get eternal peace. The right leg is firmly resting on the dwarf demon *muyalakan,* who symbolizes spiritual ignorance. The snake around his neck represents the *Kundalini Shakthi* and the *Crescent* represents the feminine energy that churns life in the world. The eternal river Ganga runs through his spread-out *kesham, hair* just as she meanders through various parts of India.'

'Lord Shiva showcases the eternal Cosmos, the cycle of life, the path to end suffering and achieve eternal salvation, all in one single pose of Nataraja.'

'*Om Nama Shivaya*,' concluded Muruga.

The entourage, including Senguntha, and Deva were stunned with the depth of knowledge that Muruga possessed. Everyone could see godliness in this divine child.

After worshipping Lord Shiva at *Thillai,* the platoon moved on further south. It was dusk when they reached the river bank of *Manniyaaru or* manni river which was a tributary of the Cauvery.

'Muruga, shall we set up camp here for the night on the banks of the river. It would be a comfortable place for us to eat and drink. Additionally, we will also have the cool breeze from the river to have a peaceful sleep at night,' said Deva.

'Yes, Deva, I agree. The troops have travelled quite a bit and its best to camp now for them to rest and rejuvenate, we still have a long way to go,' said Muruga.

'Muruga, I have a suggestion,' said Deva. Muruga nodded his head as if to say, go ahead.

'We have embarked on a long journey just like Lord Rama. He was Dharma personified; you are on the path to restore Dharma. I feel we should leave behind a *kalvettu, stone inscription* to showcase your path to the future generations.

Rama's journey became the Ramayanam, may be your path will also become a sacred book in the future.'

'Deva, I am not the creator of the path of Dharma. I am merely a traveller on it, treading the path of righteousness. Great incarnations who lived in different Yugas have already shown us the way,' said Muruga.

'Muruga, for us who are suffering, we see you as a *manitha deivam, human god,*' said Deva with a sense of devotion.

'Deva, if it makes you and the people happy, I see it as the wish of Lord Mahadev. Please go ahead,' said Muruga.

An extremely pleased Deva, marked the place for a *kalvettu*. Just then Muruga noticed there was a light flickering nearby; it seemed like a temple.

'Deva, is that a temple nearby?' asked Muruga. Yes, it is a temple of sorts,' replied Deva.

'Legend has it that there was a test of strength between *Adiseshan*, the coiled snake on whom Lord Vishnu rests and *Vayu, the Wind God*. Adiseshan was to hold on to Meru Mountain while Vayu tried to blow it away with his strength. During the tug of war, a small piece of the mountain is said to have broken away and fallen here, which created the mound. Since it's a *Swayambhu, self- manifested*, the locals worship it as Lord Shiva, as he is the only Swayambhu. The mound is called Sathya Giri,' concluded Deva.

'Don't forget I am the son of a Swayambhu too,' said Muruga with a smirk.

'It is such a coincidence that we have set up camp in this place. Two celestial beings had tested their strength against each other. I am going to test mine against a great Asura.'

'I would like to pray here to Lord Shiva.'

Muruga took water from the nearby Manni River and used it to perform the rituals to Lord Shiva. He prayed to the Supreme Lord to give him the necessary strength and courage to fight Sooran in the mother of all battles.

As Muruga was intensely worshipping Lord Shiva, he had a vision; Lord Shiva was pointing to the base of the mound that Muruga was worshipping. He continued to be in a state of trance till there was a reverberation on the earth. It looked like a mini earthquake. It startled everyone except Muruga. He calmly got up from his prayers and saw there was a crack that had formed from the base of the mound outwards. A bright light was emanating from the crack that intrigued

Muruga, he went near and saw a shiny arrow inside it. He took it out with reverence and saw an inscription in it. It was a drawing of a cow followed by a crown. Deva and Senguntha came running towards Muruga as he held the arrow in his hand.

'Senguntha, do you know the meaning of the inscription?' asked Muruga.

Senguntha said, 'You are the *gnana panditha,* you tell us.'

'The inscription shows two figures a *pashu* and a *kireedam*. It denotes that this belongs to the Lord of all living beings or *Pashupathi,* who is none other than Lord Shiva,' said Muruga.

He immediately took the shiny arrow to his eyes as a mark of respect.

'*Har Har Mahadev,*' bellowed the entire platoon.

'Muruga, Lord Shiva has answered your prayers and blessed you with a weapon. We will mark this place as *Kumara Puram* in the *kalvettu.* Maybe someone in the future might also be rewarded like you, when they pray here,' said Deva.

'Deva, Lord Shiva grants their wish to anyone who prays with unconditional devotion. It's just providence that I am here in this place.'

The platoon was on its way once again towards their final destination. As they headed further south, they came near the town of Thiruparankunram, a place historically known for the *Pancha Pandava* caves. It was believed that the Pandavas along with Draupadi lived in these caves. Just as the platoon neared the caves, a few hermits accosted Muruga and the platoon.

'Lord, we are Shiva *bhaktas* and we live in these caves. We worship *Umai Andar,* Lord of Uma. We believe you are on a holy mission,' said the hermits and placed their hands on Muruga's head as a blessing.

Muruga bowed his head in reverence. Hermits who are staunch Shiva *bhaktas* were most revered, as they had dedicated their entire life to chanting his name without even food or water for several days.

'*Shivan adiyargale,*' said Muruga in chaste Sangam Tamil language. 'We would be very happy if you could accompany us in our holy mission. Your power of prayer with the power of Pasupathi's weapon, will help us succeed,' he concluded, bowing to them once again.

Thiruchitrambalam! Thiruchitrambalam! said the hermits, which meant it was God's will and they would bow down to it.

The entourage started their journey once again. They had traversed half a day before they reached the southernmost part of India. They had reached Senthilpuri, a beautiful location near the Bay of Bengal. The place was very tranquil. Muruga heard a voice in his head and decided to drop anchor.

'Deva, I have reached my destination. This would be our base camp. Let us set up permanent structures in this place for our army and us. In the future, this place would probably witness great celebration. The celebration, of good over evil,' said Muruga, as if he had a premonition.

'Muruga, we will create a brilliant palace where you will reside. Vishwakarman, who is our chief architect, has been travelling with us all this while, specifically for this purpose,' said an elated Deva.

'The mini town we create here will remain for thousands of years. It shall showcase the art and engineering of our clan and also the sacred abode of Lord Muruga, the saviour of Suras and the restorer of Dharma,' concluded Deva with a sense of pride.

A wonderfully sea-facing abode with two floors was created by Vishwakarman and his team. It had the beauty of bamboo on the windows and walls built from solid rocks. There was a wooden staircase from within the house that would allow the occupants to climb to the terrace. A scenic view of the sea under the moonlight awaited the inmates of the abode. It was indeed a great piece of architecture.

Muruga was so pleased with his abode, he lay on the terrace viewing the stars and contemplating, *'What a peaceful place, the sound of the waves under the moonlight. Why are people fighting for petty things when nature has so much to offer,'* he said to himself.

It was dinner time and Muruga walked down the wooden steps, to join Senguntha and Deva who were waiting for him.

'Deva, why don't you tell me about the Asura clan, since you have been at war with them. I want to understand their mind and see if I can mend their ways,' said Muruga.

'Muruga, you are the son of a great master. You know a great deal. I may not be able to tell you the nuances of human behaviour,' said Deva.

'Doesn't matter, Deva, just tell me about their ancestry, and I will read between your lines and figure it out,' said Muruga nonchalantly.

'Looks like we will have a long night...,'said Deva with a sigh.

'Deva, our scriptures say *'thamasoma jyothirgamaya,' lead us from the darkness to the light*. The long night today could well decide if you will see the light of the day in the future,' said Muruga with a smirk.

THE ASURA LEGACY

Deva's narrative unfolded like the pages of an ancient manuscript, revealing the intricate tapestry of Asura history. Muruga listened intently, absorbing the tales of ambition, betrayal, and redemption that shaped the destiny of the Asura clan.

Asurendra founded the Asura clan. He married Mangalakesi, and they had a daughter named Surasai. The guru of the Asuras was Shukra. He was the greatest sorcerer of his times. He taught Surasai all the sorcery he knew. Even as a young child, Surasai had picked up nuances of sorcery and wizardry. Shukra was very pleased with his disciple, so he nicknamed her Maya. It was an apt name for her, as she was an illusion in many ways.

Asurendra had lost several battles to Surendra, the forefather of the Sura clan, and to Sundara. Thus, they lived a secluded life. Their pride was severely hurt, and they couldn't do much. Shukra wanted the Asuras to succeed and his only ray of hope was Maya.

Maya was beauty personified, shrewd, and the queen of sorcery. It is believed that Shukra had asked Maya to entice Sage Kashyapa and beget children through him, so they would acquire great knowledge from the sage and inherit wizardry through Maya. They would be humans with a heady mix of knowledge, power and sorcery. This would help them take anyone head-on.

Maya bought into this plan. She figured out that Sage Kashyapa was in *Meru Malai or Mount Meru* which was in the northern-most part of India. Deciding to traverse the length of the country, she set out to complete her mission. When the task was about restoring the pride of the clan, nothing would stop Maya.

She finally met Sage Kashyapa. He was smitten by her beauty and lost track of his penance. He started inquiring about her. She disregarded him stating that he was a sage and he shouldn't be looking at women and talking to them. Kashyapa told her that his penance had been answered. Maya walked away nonchalantly, and disappeared within seconds. A distraught Kashyapa couldn't continue his penance nor could he forget this maiden. At dusk, Maya reappeared in front of him. Kashyapa was happy to see her back and asked her to be his partner.

Maya agreed to be his partner on one condition: that they would consummate only at a time and place that she decides. Kashyapa, who was intoxicated with *kama* simply shook his head to everything that Maya said.

That night in the *muthal jamam, first of the three-hour* night cycle. They consummated and soon after a male child was born. She named him Padhman a word associated with the lotus, one which is pure even when it rises from the dirt. The lotus also signified rebirth in the old scriptures. She believed her boy would give rebirth to the Asuras as the greatest clan, the world has ever seen. She knew her methods may be impure, but her intent was to bestow glory to her clan.

Padhman is none other than Sooran.

A year after Padhman was born, in the *erendaam jamam, second of the three-hour night cycle*, she consummated with Kashyapa and their second child was born. She named him Simhan, the lion-hearted, the one who would be the bravest and attain leadership qualities.

A year after Simhan was born, in the *moondraam jamam, the third hour of the three-hour* night cycle, she consummated again with Kashyapa and their third child was born. She named him Tharakan, the star. He being the youngest, became the apple of her eye and the star of the family.

'Muruga, it is the same Tharakan that you obliterated in the *Krauncha Malai* war,' said Deva and paused to drink a glass of somapanam.

'Whether you are a sage or simpleton, when blinded by Maya, you will go astray. When you are born in darkness and live in darkness with no spiritual inkling, you will continue to eternally remain in the cycle of life driven by petty materialistic objects. Sooran needs a spiritual awakening, and I shall provide that to him,' said Muruga.

Deva now continued his narration.

Padhman, Simhan and Tharakan were taught scriptures by their father Kashyapa. They became very staunch devotees of Lord Shiva and would meditate most of the time. Meanwhile, Maya taught them sorcery and the use of weapons.

When they grew up to be young and powerful lads, Kashyapa asked them to focus their life on doing good and spreading Shaivism across the length and breadth of the country. Maya differed with Kashyapa, arguing that he was a hermit, not them. They were knowledgeable and powerful wizards and should use their skills to conquer the world, else they would be wasting their life. Kashyapa by now realized Maya's ulterior motives and left the place forever. He didn't wish to be part of their evil actions.

Maya advised her three children to have the goal of achieving greatness in life. She urged them to make use of their knowledge as well as sorcery and pray to Lord Shiva with flesh and blood by following the tantric practices that she had taught them. She desired an end state, where any human or animal would dread the name Asura. Asuras should never have to bow down to anyone ever again.

Sooran and his brothers proceeded on their journey south. Their first pit stop was at their *kula guru, the spiritual leader* of their clan, Shukra. Shukra was very pleased to see mighty Padhman. Padhman narrated to Shukra, what he had learnt from Kashyapa and Maya, and sought his advice. Shukra was pleased that his disciple Maya had taught her sons well. He urged them to fulfil their mothers wishes. He taught them the *Maha Mrityunjay Mantra* also known as *Rudra Mantra, prayer to Lord Rudra.* This prayer is to attain a state of deathlessness. He urged Sooran to do penance to Lord Rudra through his *Velvi, sacrifice and offering.* Sooran was now extremely enthused, having got the blessings of his *kula guru.*

Sooran and his brothers continued their travel for a long period of time, and reached a place called *Aalankadu.* He decided that this would be the location, where he would perform the greatest *Velvi* that would please Lord Rudra. In the tantric practices, Goddess Kali is considered the recipient of the sacrifices which was blood and flesh. She is considered the *Adi Shakthi, the primordial force.* He created two thousand *yaaga kundams, fire pits,* where the offerings would be done to please Goddess Kali and Lord Rudra. He and his brothers closeted themselves for several years to build their power of illusion, physical strength, and ability to control weapons with their mind. To achieve this, it needed tremendous self-control, dedication, focus, patience, grit and self-belief. Sooran reached a point where he was ready to self-immolate himself if he didn't achieve this *siddhi, success.*

Once they came out of *Aalankadu,* there was no stopping them. The three brothers now went on a rampage, taking over village after village and spreading fear and terror among common people. The ones who were well-built were inducted into the army and made into ruthless mercenaries who would kill for Sooran just by looking at his hand gesture. Asuras created many tyrants and sent them all over, to capture kingdom after kingdom and every clan. The clans became submissive to them once they accepted Sooran as their *Chakravarthi, Supreme Emperor.* The Danavas, Daityas, and Nagas became part of the Asura clan. The only ones whom the Asuras left alone were the Ganas, as they were considered direct descendants of Lord Mahadev. Deva now paused again to drink another gulp of somapanam; the mere talk of Sooran made his tongue go dry.

'Deva, I am really fascinated by Sooran; he has attained great siddhi, but is using it for the wrong purpose. How many children spend their entire lifetime in fulfilling their mothers' wishes and bring glory to their motherland and their clan. Sooran is a selfless individual who has inner light but is blinded by the glory of power. I await the day when I would meet him face to face,' said Muruga with a gleeful expression.

'Muruga, there is more complexity to the Asura Legacy. Kashyapa had multiple wives; one of them was Aditi, my mother. In a way, Sooran and I are stepbrothers. Shakti's stepsister Diti also married Kashyapa and created the Daitya clan. In a way, you are related to the Asuras too from your mother's side,' concluded Deva.

'So, this is in a way a kind of war between brothers. It reminds me of the Mahabharat. It looks like this cycle of brother against brother will continue for several centuries to come,' said Muruga.

'Deva, why does Sooran have so much hatred towards Suras in particular, and wants their complete decimation,' asked Muruga.

'Muruga, we have been taught the methods of finding water, creating fire and harnessing air. Asuras know that these are the vital ingredients to sustain the life of all the people. This makes them dependent on us. The constant effort of Asurendra was to take over the Sura clan, and control these critical activities so he becomes the supreme controller of life. We however are governed by Lord Shiva and only perform our duties as prescribed to us. Since we provide all these vital ingredients, we get paid by every clan, hence it makes us rich,' concluded Deva.

'Deva, quick question to you: do you distribute your riches among the poor and needy, whether they belong to your clan or others?' asked Muruga.

'Muruga...ah ah..., Deva stuttered and then answered, no, Muruga we don't. Every clan has to fend for itself.'

'Wealth begets pride, pride begets arrogance. Life always balances itself. What goes up has to come down. Asuras have placed you in this position so that you can understand, what it means to be without wealth and the pride that comes with it,' said Muruga.

Deva bowed his head in shame. Muruga though younger than him, had an invisible halo around him that engulfed everyone, who was in his presence.

'Deva, continue and complete what you started, so we finish it and get a good night's sleep,' said Muruga.

Sooran, after bringing all major clans under his control, set his eyes on *Alakapuri,* the kingdom of Vaisravana, the richest man on the planet. Vaisravana knew the powers that Sooran now possessed. He welcomed him with open arms and pledged that all his wealth would be at the service of Sooran. With Vaisravana's wealth, Sooran added more weapons to his armoury. Sooran amassed the largest army and went after your uncle. He tried to fight Sooran but in vain and surrendered. Sooran pardoned him as he was the brother-in-law of Swayambhu. Sooran marched to the smaller kingdom run by Prajwal, and defeated him with ease. Pawan went into hiding and so did I. The once mighty court of Indraprastha had an empty throne.

Sooran had conquered all the major clans, so he had to be anointed the King of Kings. Prajapathi and Sundara suggested that the Suras seek pardon from Sooran and not remain in hiding. Sundara decided that he would play the role of peacemaker. Sundara told Sooran that he should pardon the Suras and allow them to lead a normal life. Sooran agreed to Sundara's suggestion, and the Suras lived to fight another day.

A grand city called *Veera Mahendrapuri* was created by Vishwakarman on the edge of the ocean in the southern peninsula. The location was suggested by Shukra. Several islands were created in the sea to host the soldiers of the vast Asura army. In the areas adjoining *Veera Mahendrapuri,* several towns were created which would host the sub-clans of the Asuras.

On the day of Sooran's coronation as *Chakravarthi*, Prajapathi did the honours by crowning Sooran. I held the *thamboolam, a basket of betel leaf & nut* carried as part of the rituals during any auspicious occasion, while Pawan kept Sooran cool with the *venchaamaram, an ornamental fan.* Our humiliation was complete.

'Muruga, I am exhausted physically and mentally. I would like to take my leave now,' said Deva and left in a hurry.

WRATH OF BANUKOBAN

Early next morning, Senguntha and Deva met Muruga during breakfast. After finishing it, they went around the islands to oversee the training of the warriors. Even if there wasn't a war, they had to keep themselves sharp. After an hour the trio returned to Muruga's abode.

'Deva, it looks like I touched a wrong chord yesterday by asking too many details about the legacy of the Asuras,' said Muruga.

'Not at all, you are the supreme commander of the forces and it is important that you understand the background of the enemy. Overnight I realized my folly. As our saviour, you are entitled to all possible information about your opponent, and it is my duty to provide you with as much detail as I can,' said Deva, his hands folded in a *namaskaram* and head bowed down.

'As long as it doesn't upset you, I am happy to hear more of Sooran's back story,' said Muruga.

Deva continued where he left off the previous night.

Sooran had made a truce with the Suras with the help of Prajapathi and Sundar, however, he continued to harass the Suras. We were made to pay more taxes and do menial errands for the Asuras. It was nothing short of slavery.

Just like the *Agyathavasam, the period of living in hiding* that the pandavas had to go through, the Suras went into hiding. I was living near Seerkazhi with my family. Prajwal, Pawan and Varun were all living in islands away from our motherland. Sooran wanted to humiliate the Suras even after pardoning us. He sent his troops all over to search for us. We somehow survived the search and continued to live as nomads.

One day a few of the members of the Sura community found my hideout and came to see me. They begged that I reach out to Swayambhu and seek a solution. They couldn't endure the slavery anymore. I couldn't see my people suffering, so I decided to come out of hiding and meet Lord Swayambhu. Sachi fainted on hearing that I wanted to go and meet Lord Swayambhu. She feared the worst, but I was able to convince her and make the journey.

Our troubles were about to worsen. Sachi shared with me the ordeal she had gone through in Seerkazhi. To ensure that I succeed in the task I had undertaken, Sachi prayed to Lord Mahadev, inside the bamboo forest near Seerkazhi where we were in hiding.

Ajamukhi, Soora's sister and her friend Dhunmukhi were travelling across the land for their lustful pleasures. They happened to hear the sounds of '*Om Nama Shivaya*' and ventured into the bamboo forest and saw Sachi in intense prayer.

'*Ha Ha Ha*!' A reverberating laughter filled the air.

'You swine, you are here and your husband is hiding somewhere else. You are wasting your time with that impotent man. Come with me and I shall take you to my brother Sooran. He is the *Chakravarthi*; the king of kings and he will make you the chief queen. You will forget your husband and the Suras in no time and would yearn for that life in your future births too,' bellowed Ajamukhi.

Sachi got angry and cursed Ajamukhi that she was behaving worse than a pimp. An enraged Ajamukhi started dragging Sachi by her hair. A helpless Sachi hugged the Shiva Lingam she was praying to and cried out to Lord Shiva for help. A dark man with a big moustache and a long beard with *vibuthi* smeared on his forehead burst through the bamboo forest. He screamed at Ajamukhi to let go of the Shiva devotee, Ajamukhi spat on him and continued to drag Sachi with her. The bearded man warned Ajamukhi of dire consequences.

Ajamukhi laughed and said, 'You look like a *pithan*, a *madman*. I am the sister of Sooran. You would be foolish to attack me.' and continued to drag Sachi. The Dark Man's eyes turned red and in one sweeping stroke, he cut off Ajamukhi's hand. Writhing in pain Ajamukhi fled the place holding her severed hand. Sachi thanked the Dark man and inquired about his identity. He introduced himself as Maha Kaalan. Sachi bowed to him. She felt that Lord Shiva had arrived in human form to save her. Maha Kaalan remained a guardian to Sachi till I returned.

Deva paused to drink a glass of Somapanam to quench the thirst of his parched throat.

'I am eager to know what happened next,' said Muruga with a sense of anticipation etched on his face.

'I will verbatim tell you what happened in Sooran's court just like Prajapathi told me; he was a witness to the proceedings. I felt I was watching Ramayana 2.0 unfold in front of me,' said Deva and continued.

Ajamukhi came crying into the court with a *perum olam, a loud wail.* With tears in her eyes and blood on her hands, she looked at Sooran.

'You are the king of kings and look what has happened to your sister. Sachi was hiding in Seerkazhi. I wanted to bring her as a slave to you, so you could do as you please but a bearded stooge of the Suras, cut my hand. It is a disgrace to the Asura clan. If you don't decimate every single Sura and their puppets, the world will laugh at you. She now turned her attention to Simhan and Tharakan. I have three brothers whom the world fears and yet I have been humiliated brutally,' and let out a deafening cry in despair.

Sooran seethed with rage and vowed to kill every single Sura and their supporters. He screamed at the top of his voice and everyone in the courtroom dreaded the consequence. Just then, in a calm demeanour his son Banukoban stood up with folded hands in namaskaram.

'*Appa*, the man doesn't seem like a petty warrior who supports the Suras. There is no one in their entire clan who dare do such an act. Allow me to restore the Asura clan's legacy. I will find this bearded man and decapitate him. I will ensure every Sura pays with their blood for every drop of blood that my aunt has spilled,' said Banukoban pointing his hands towards Ajamukhi.

Sooran was filled with pride and asked Prajapathi who was seated in the court to provide the auspicious time for his son to go on this mission. Prajapathi looked at the *panchangam, almanac* and provided the appropriate date and time for Banukoban to leave for his mission.

As planned, Banukoban arrived in Seerkazhi with the help of Dhunmukhi and went into the bamboo forest. Neither Sachi nor the bearded man were present. Filled with rage, Banukoban decided to plunder Indraprastha.

'One of the Suras, who witnessed the battle between Banukoban and Jayanthan narrated to me what happened at Indraprastha and I shall relay it verbatim,' said Deva and continued,

Jayanthan, my son was at Indraprastha as the royal representative to help the Suras. News reached Jayanthan that Banukoban was on his way to destroy Indraprastha. Jayanthan decided it was time for retribution. He gathered the Sura troops and decided to fight Banukoban.

Jayanthan took the Sura army to the outpost of Indraprastha. Sura troops consisted of both the military personnel and civilians. Ordinary citizens of Indraprastha also decided to wield weapons against the Asuras. Banukoban was taken aback by the sudden transformation of the timid Suras.

The troops of Suras and Asuras were now face to face against each other. According to Dharmic principles of war, Banukoban sounded his bugle to indicate that they were ready for battle. Jayanthan took out his conch and blew to signal that they were prepared for war too.

'Banukoba, your fight is with us. Let's leave the people out of it,' said Jayanthan.

'I don't want to show my Valor on innocent people either,' replied Banukoban.

My Lord, give me the opportunity to fight this battle,' said Neelakesan bowing his head in front of Banukoban. Neelakesan was Banukoban's trusted lieutenant.

'May victory be yours, go ahead,' said Banukoban.

Neelakesan underestimated Jayanthan's ability. Even though the Suras had lost their war with Sooran, they were still fierce warriors. It was a fight unto death with arrows.

Neelakesan sent a flurry of arrows towards Jayanthan, who countered them with his own set of arrows. The battle raged on for an hour. Neelakesan was losing his strength. Jayanthan who noticed that his opponent was fatigued, started to impose himself and increased the rate at which he sent his arrows across, one of them broke Neelakesan bow. By the time he picked up another bow, a flurry of arrows pierced his chest and stomach.

Neelakesan feel down with a thump and died an instant death.

With Neelakesan dead, it was time for Banukoban to enter the battle. Banukoban was no ordinary warrior. Beyond his ability with various weapons, he was a master of deception and illusion, that he had learnt from Shukra. Jayanthan was no match for him.

'You are a good warrior. Not bad at all Jayantha,' said Banukoban.

He lifted his bow and sent a flurry of arrows that broke Jayanthan's chariot and removed his crown. A disoriented Jayanthan fell to the ground. Banukoban waited for him to rise. Jayanthan got up and released a set of arrows which Banukoban easily parried away. He released a couple of arrows in quick succession and one of them pierced Jayanthan's shoulder. Jayanthan lost hold of his bow and fell to the ground. He lay there for a moment, now a sitting duck for Banukoban.

He could hear the Asuras shouting kill him, burn him. He thought his end would come soon.

'Stop it! said a booming voice, he fought a brave battle. He doesn't deserve to die this way,' said Banukoban.

Jayanthan was pleasantly surprised by the approach of Sooran's son.

Banukoban ordered his warriors to take Jayanthan and the rest of the Asuras captive.

'Burn Indraprastha down, with it the Suras pride will burn too,' commanded Banukoban.

Jayanthan and other Suras were produced before Sooran. 'Every Sura was mutilated before being thrown in the cellar to avenge Ajamukhi,' said Deva and broke down.

Muruga too felt Deva's pain and consoled Deva who was now weeping profusely.

MESSAGE TO MAHENDRAPURI

The next day brought a new dawn in more ways than one. Over the last two days, the chosen one had delved into the history of the Asuras seeking to understand the origins of the rivalry with the Suras and the suffering they had endured.

'Senguntha, gather all the warriors and assemble them on the beach. I would like to address them,' Muruga instructed.

Within an hour, the entire beach stretch of Senthilpuri was filled with a sea of humanity, Muruga's warriors were eager to listen to their commander.

'*Thozhargale,*' *dear friends,* I empathize with the deep pain experienced by the Suras. I am also aware that my father has treated members of both clans as his own children. When a child goes rogue, it is important to exercise the four-step process as described in our ancient scriptures- *saama, dhaana, bedha, dhandam,* to bring the child back on the right track.'

Saama: Providing an opportunity for the child to correct its mistake by explaining the ill effects of the blunder.

Dhaana: Providing positive compensation to the child in lieu of not committing the blunder again.

Bedha: Grounding the child.

Dhandam: Physical punishment if the child continues to misbehave.

'Be it a child or an enemy, the first step is to pardon and provide an opportunity to change; that is true dharma,' concluded Muruga.

The entire army shouted '*Aro Hara!*' in unison, conveying their agreement to Muruga's proposition.

'Deva, we need to send a messenger to Mahendrapuri to inform Sooran that he will be pardoned for his sins if he releases Jayanthan and the rest of the Suras,' stated Muruga.

'Muruga, none of the Suras would be allowed inside Mahendrapuri. We are deemed to be slaves and will be captured the moment we set foot on their land,' replied Deva.

'If that's the case, who do you suggest should undertake this crucial mission?' Muruga inquired.

'In my humble opinion, the mighty Senguntha would be the best candidate to carry out this mission. He has courage, conviction, and wisdom. Above all, he has your blessings,' said Deva.

'Senguntha, I agree with Deva. Go to Mahendrapuri, ask Sooran to release the prisoners. If he doesn't agree, explain the consequences to him,' Muruga directed.

'*Ayyane, My Lord*. It is my honour that you have chosen me for this mission. With your blessings, I will accomplish the task and return successfully,' said Senguntha and bent down to touch Muruga's feet. Muruga lifted him up and hugged him.

'Your place is in my heart, not at my feet,' said Muruga and wished him good luck.

Senguntha turned to the warriors and said 'I will be back soon to celebrate Sooran's surrender. However, keep your minds and weapons sharp; we may need to go to war if the need arises.'

Bidding goodbye to the soldiers and Deva, Senguntha departed on his mission. It was reminiscent of Angad's journey to King Ravana's court.

Senguntha strode like a colossus on his horse with his sword firmly tucked in its scabbard. He rode northwards and reached a place called *Gandha Madhana Parvatham,* a hillock that had become famous as the locals believed it had Lord Rama's feet on it. It was close to Rameshwaram, where Rama had prayed to Lord Shiva before taking on the mighty Ravana.

Senguntha stopped and prayed at the hillock dedicated to Lord Rama, the most righteous king this country had ever seen. '*Let Lord Rudra give me the same strength he gave you,*' said Senguntha to himself, with his eyes closed.

From there, he journeyed to the lands' end where he had to cross the Southern Ocean. Hiring a boat near Danushkoti, literally meaning Land's End, he proceeded towards the town of Lanka Pattinam, following the path of the Rama Sethu. Situated at the northernmost part of Mahendrapuri, Lanka Pattinam was the first obstacle in reaching Sooran's Kingdon. Sooran had organized his kingdom in such a way that it resembled the *Chakravyuham, a military formation of concentric circles* to trap the enemy. Even if one were to come through, they would find it very difficult to get out.

Lanka Pattinam was guarded by one of Sooran's trusted lieutenants, *Yaali Mugan*. No one had seen his face as he always had the mask of the mythological creature *Yaali*, which had a lion's face and the trunk and tusks of an elephant. It was considered a creature of protection. In this case, Yaali Mugan was the protector of Sooran and his kingdom. Fortunately for Senguntha, Yaali Mugan had gone to Mahendrapuri to see Sooran. He left his son Adhi Veeran and the commander-in-chief, Veera Singha Mugan, in charge of Lanka Pattinam.

As Senguntha rode in front of the main fortress of Lanka Pattinam, he was confronted by Veera Singha Mugan.

'You look like a seasoned warrior, but you seem to have come in the wrong direction. Turn around and leave,' said Veera Singha Mugan.

'I am on a mission to meet Sooran in Mahendrapuri. Please don't waste my time,' said Senguntha.

'Have you have lost your mind? You have no idea what you are saying and to whom.'

'Guards! Arrest this impudent man and throw him in the cellar,' screamed Veera.

'I thought you are a brave man like me. Turns out that you are a sheep in wolf's clothing,' said Senguntha with a smirk.

'Well, you seem to have a death wish. I shall certain grant that to you,' said Veera and let out a huge roar of laughter.

Both warriors patted their horses and signalled to them to go back. The horses trudged backward slowly. Both warriors paused. Then, as if on cue, they charged towards each other. Senguntha was swirling his knife, in both directions while galloping on his horse. The two warriors clashed when they were next to each other. The horses crossed over and stopped after running a short distance. Veera's hands dropped to the ground, blood pouring profusely from his shoulders.

The rest of the warriors lost their morale to fight, and ran to Adhi Veeran to inform him, that a maniac warrior was at their gate. Adhi Veeran strode out on a dazzling white horse. He was a charming young man.

'Who are you? How dare you cut off the hands of my commander?' screamed Adhi Veeran.

'Young man, I am Senguntha, the second-in-command of Muruga's Army. I am his messenger and on my way to Mahendrapuri to meet Sooran.'

'It is not in our principle to fight a messenger, but you have committed a crime in our land and you shall be punished,' said Adhi Veeran very sternly.

'Charge!' he screamed to his personal body guards. Ten of them surrounded Senguntha.

In a flash, Senguntha jumped from his horse and scythed through the head of one of the guards with his sword. As he landed, he spun like a top and severed their lower limbs in a flash. All of them were immobilized, unable to fight.

'Let me go now,' said Senguntha to Adhi Veeran.

'Oh, brave warrior, it is my duty to guard my land. I will fight to the death,' said Adhi Veeran.

'I salute you, young man,' said Senguntha.

Adhi Veeran got down from his horse and ran towards Senguntha with his sword. A fierce battle ensued between the two. Adhi Veeran lunged forward with a swift thrust, aiming for Senguntha's chest. Senguntha sidestepped and countered with a sweeping slash towards Adhi Veeran's exposed side. Senguntha landed precise strikes that gradually wore down Adhi Veeran's defenses.

With every attack Adhi Veeran made, Senguntha would cut through some part of Adhi Veeran's body. The young man was no match for him. However, Adhi Veeran refused to yield, driven by pride and duty to protect his motherland, even though he was bleeding from every part of his body. A heavily wounded Adhi Veeran continued to fight with whatever little ounce of strength he had in him. Senguntha decided to end Adhi Veeran's torture. With one swirl of his sword, he severed Adhi Veeran's head. As the headless body fell to the earth, Senguntha bent down and whispered into the ears of the bodyless head that rolled onto the other side, 'Muruga blesses your soul.'

There was an eerie silence as Senguntha mounted his horse, and rode through Lanka Pattinam. It resembled a ghost town. All the citizens had locked themselves up, fearing the wrath of a fearsome warrior. News had spread thick and fast that this warrior had killed their crown prince and mutilated their commander-in-chief so badly that he would remain a disabled man for life. Senguntha traversed the length of the city uninterrupted and strode gallantly towards Mahendrapuri, the land of Sooran, the Supreme Lord of the Asuras.

RENDEZVOUS WITH SOORAN

Jayanthan was before a Shiva Lingam, his hands held together in prayer and tears flowing down his eyes with a prayer on his lips.

'Oh Mahadev, how long do we have to go through this ordeal? There is no end in sight. You swallowed poison for the benefit of others, would you not show some mercy towards us?'

A flash of light appeared above the Shiva lingam. In it was a man on a chariot with a spear to his side, with OM inscribed on it in Sangam Tamil. Jayanthan was startled awake on his cell floor. The moment he got up, the pain from the previous night's torture started setting in again. There was a belief that early morning dreams come true.

Uncertain of its meaning, he shared the vision with his close aides from the Sura clan, who were also locked up in the heavily guarded prison of Veera Mahendrapuri. Was it just an illusion, or was someone coming their way to release them from captivity? At the very least, it seemed like a good omen.

Far away, Senguntha approached the Northern gates of Mahendrapuri. The grandeur of the gates stunned him. Senguntha said to himself, *'Oru paanai sotrukku oru soru padham.'* It meant that a morsel of rice was good enough to know if the rice is cooked. The mere entrance of Mahendrapuri reflected the majestic nature of the city. He stopped at a fair distance and moved under a tree, where he could get a good view of the infantry protecting the gates. There were men on horses moving back and forth. There were warriors on top of elephants standing guard on either side. There were chariots near the entrance for emergencies. As he was watching the action in front of him, a small portion of the door opened, and out walked two identical men. They were the chief guardians of the Northern gates, Goran and Agoran.

With the armour around them and their crowns, they appeared like giants among men. An impressed Senguntha decided to check out the other gates.

At an opportune moment around noon, when the changeovers were happening, Senguntha rode towards the southern gate. Here again, he stopped at a distance, dismounted, and watched the people around the gates. The sight was very similar; horses, elephants, and warriors guarding the gates. He knew that there would be chief guardians here too. Just then, he heard the soldiers greeting the warlords. Senguntha understood that Mahendrapuri was an extremely fortified city. He silently moved towards the eastern entrance.

Senguntha waited on the sidelines, watching the activities on the eastern side. Everything seemed to be similar to the Northern and Southern sides but less in number. Would they let him inside if they knew he was a messenger, or would they haul him into the dungeon, assuming he was a Sura warrior? While Senguntha was lost in thought, he felt a tap on his shoulder. The tap felt more like a slap. He turned around to see a giant man in an elephant mask, known as Gaja Mugan in these parts. He looked like a tusker that was about to charge.

'You seem to be stealthily looking around. You are a Sura spy, aren't you?' barked the masked man.

'I am no spy but I am a warrior. I am prepared to fight you, if you wish,' retorted Senguntha.

'Fight me?' said the masked man with a huge roar of laughter.

'You can call for help, if you need support to fight me,' said Senguntha with a smirk.

An enraged Gaja Mugan tried to crush Senguntha with his bare hands. Senguntha bent down in time and struck him below the belt where it hurts the most. The masked man writhed in pain and fell on his knees. In a flash, Senguntha swung behind him and slit his throat. Knowing chaos would ensue soon, he sped away from the scene and hid himself in an abandoned house.

After night fall, Senguntha approached the eastern gate, where the guards were relatively fewer compared to the other gates. Using a rope and hook, he climbed over the wall where there was no light. He could see huge buildings, palaces, and elegant pavements. He couldn't believe his eyes. He felt that the Asuras lived like there was no tomorrow. He noticed one particular building which was heavily guarded. Instinctively, he knew it was the prison, the place where Jayanthan and other Suras were kept as prisoners. He decided to find a way to enter the prison so he could inform Jayanthan and other Suras that their ordeal would soon be over. Senguntha quickly scaled down the wall, jumped on top of his horse and sped away.

The next day, very early in the morning, dressed as a commoner, he went inside the eastern gate and stood opposite the prison to watch the activities. He noticed that a bullock cart with food had arrived in front of the gate. A brilliant idea flashed in his mind. He followed the bullock cart as it left the prison. It went to the house where the lunch was being prepared for the mid-day meal. He found that three people carried the meal and loaded it on to the bullock cart. One of them had gone to relieve himself. Senguntha followed him and covered his nose with a white cloth. The man fainted. Senguntha managed to get *mandragora* from the dark alleys of the city. An herb popular in the Mediterranean, it was a powerful anesthetic. It was called *kadal jaathi* in these parts. He hid the man behind bushes and reached the lunch home. He begged the boss of the lunch home for a job. Seeing a well-built man, the boss asked him to load the food onto the bullock cart and drive it to the prison.

Senguntha happily got to work and left for the prison. A small bottle of *mandragora* was tucked into his *veshti's* folds. It would prove useful later. After reaching the prison, as the food was being unloaded, Senguntha befriended one of the guards and told him he had special meat to be delivered to him. He took him aside to give the special gift. Before the guard could realize, Senguntha covered the guard's nose with a cloth he was carrying, and the guard passed out. Senguntha raised an alarm, and other guards rushed into check on their colleague. Using the commotion as a distraction, Senguntha looked into the cell and saw a shining young man in front of him. He knew that was Jayanthan. He called out and handed over a palm leaf to him. It read *'Yaam Irukka Bayam Yen'* and had an illustration of a spear.

'I have arrived. Muruga will follow soon,' said Senguntha in a hushed voice.

Jayanthan knew that his dream was about to come true. The saviour was on his way.

Senguntha knew that it would be impossible to reach Sooran directly, as there were too many chieftains and Sooran's son Banukoban to contend with. He decided that stealth was the only way to gain an audience with Sooran. Knowing Sooran's penchant for riches and his desire for flaunting his wealth, Senguntha disguised himself as a trader from a faraway land with great riches. He bribed his way into Sooran's court.

Sooran was in the midst of discussion with his warlords, reviewing spy reports on the whereabouts of the Suras and the young boy who had killed his brother.

A soldier stepped in and said, *'Mannar Manna,* there is a trader from a faraway land who has the greatest diamond of all and wishes to present it to your Lordship.'

'You impudent fool! Can't you see I am busy with war plans?' screamed an angry Sooran.

The soldier stood there, shivering, unsure of what to say or do.

'Anyway, send him in. Let me see what he has,' said Sooran, now calmer.

'Greetings to the great Sooran,' said Senguntha, hands folded in *namaskaram.*

'My blessings to you trader. May you end up doing more trade with our land and keep paying my taxes. Now show me the diamond,' said Sooran with delight.

'My Lord, the diamond is with my master. He wishes to give it to you if you release Jayanthan and the other Suras,' said Senguntha nonchalantly.

'I could slay you right here for such audacity. You are no trader. Tell me the truth. Who are you?' roared an angry Sooran.

'I am the messenger of Lord Muruga, my name is Senguntha,' he replied.

'Muruga is the diamond of all diamonds. There is no one who can match his brilliance in wisdom and warfare,' said Senguntha beaming.

'So, you are the little boy's puppet,' said Sooran roaring with laughter.

'Don't be foolish. Bow to Muruga and seek his pardon, or face dire consequences,' said Senguntha sternly.

The warriors in the room all rose to attack Senguntha. Sooran raised is hands, and they stood still.

'I will spare you death as you are a messenger. Go tell that little master of yours to prepare to face my wrath,' screamed a livid Sooran.

'Looks like you haven't read our ancient scriptures. Do not under estimate someone small and young, as Mahabali did, and end up under the earth,' said Senguntha sarcastically.

'Guards! Arrest this man at once and throw him in the dungeon,' screamed Sooran.

In a flash, Senguntha swiveled and grabbed a sword from a warrior's scabbard. Spinning at furious pace, he swirled it like a discus scything through many warriors and incapacitating them. He ran out of the court room, sounded a whistle, and his horse came galloping. He mounted on it and sped away. Asura warriors began chasing him, and bugles sounded to close the main gate. Senguntha was too quick for the chasing warriors, maneuvering his way to the eastern entrance, he sped away.

Sooran was reeling from shock at what transpired in his courtroom. He cursed those near him, calling them impotent and imbecile for failing to stop a messenger from escaping.

'Appa, don't fret over a messenger's misdeeds,' said a soft voice. It was his younger son, Vajrabahu. Sooran looked at him quizzically.

'I will bring that messenger back and throw him at your feet. You decide his fate,' said Vajrabahu with great conviction.

Visibly pleased, Sooran patted his son on his back, a rare smile crossing his face, and wished him well. Sooran ordered his commanders to support Vajrabahu on his mission.

'It would be a shame if we needed an army to capture a messenger. Let me go with a few guards,' quipped Vajrabahu.

Vajrabahu left Mahendrapuri in pursuit of Senguntha.

A speeding Senguntha stopped near a pond so his horse could drink water. It was still a long way back to Senthilpuri. In many ways, the war had already started. As he contemplated the arduous journey, he heard the sound of horses neighing nearby. Realizing he was pursued, Senguntha lay still, waiting for someone to show up. Through the bushes, he saw two men charging towards him on horseback. Quickly drawing his sword from the scabbard, he ran towards them, cutting the leg of one horse, which stumbled onto the other, causing both the warriors to fall down and break their limbs.

As Senguntha watched the mayhem, a young warrior emerged from the bushes.

'Very Impressive, I've never seen a messenger with such prowess. Well done,' said Vajrabahu, clapping.

'I just happened to play the role of a messenger. I am the second-in-command of Muruga's army,' Senguntha said proudly.

'I am duty-bound to capture you and take you to my father. I give you one final chance to surrender,' said Vajrabahu with a smirk.

'Surrender is never in a warrior's lexicon. It's either victory or death,' said Senguntha, thumping his chest proudly.

Vajrabahu drew two swords from his scabbard and advanced towards Senguntha, who noted Vajrabahu's ambidexterity. Vajrabahu lunged forward swirling both swords in an attempt to inflict severe harm. Senguntha used the girdle from the fallen horse as a shield against Vajrabahu's sword and a gruesome battle ensued. Senguntha repelled every move and, in a decisive moment disarmed one of Vajrabahu's swords. Vajrabahu, undeterred, intensified his attacks with the remaining sword. With equal weapons, Senguntha upped the ante and started striking his opponent with more zest. Senguntha was impressed with the sword skills of Vajrabahu, but also noticed that the young man was tiring. This was the opportune moment to go for the kill. He swiftly moved and severed Vajrabahu's right hand.

Vajrabahu, writhing in pain, tried to pick up the sword with his lefthand, but unfortunately that was his undoing as Senguntha severed his head in one brutal blow. It was a gory end for the young son of Sooran.

Senguntha knew the stakes had escalated with the death of Sooran's son. He didn't waste any more time; he mounted his horse and sped away. He needed to cross Lanka Pattinam, take the ferry to *Gandha Madhana Parvatham* and then ride to Senthilpuri. Little did he know what awaited him in Lanka Pattinam.

As he neared the southern side of Lanka Pattinam, he was stopped by a gigantic figure. It was Yaali Mugan.

'You must be the diabolical guy who killed my son, Adhi Veeran. You shall die a dog's death,' screamed Yaali Mugan.

'Your son was a brave young man, he fought well; you should be proud of him,' said Senguntha.

'I will avenge his death by cutting you into pieces and feeding them to hungry dogs waiting in my palace,' said Yaali Mugan, grinding his teeth.

Yaali Mugan lunged forward to crush Senguntha with his bare hands. Senguntha knew he would have to use tact against his opponent. He swiftly moved to his right. Yaali Mugan uprooted a small tree near him and threw it towards Senguntha, who dodge it as he ran towards the left and jumped onto a tree. Yaali Mugan threw a huge boulder at the tree, breaking its trunk. As the tree collapsed, Senguntha balanced himself and, at the appropriate movement jumped in the air and cut off the giant's hand. Yaali Mugan screamed in pain and anger. In a swift move, Senguntha lashed out at Yaali Mugan's left leg. An imbalanced Yaali Mugan fell face down. In a flash, Senguntha was on top of Yaali Mugan, driving his sword through the rear of his neck bringing a swift end to Yaali Mugan as blood spluttered from his mouth. It was reminiscent of Balaram slaying Pralambasura.

Senguntha was now in the clear. He had killed Sooran's son and several of the warriors protecting Sooran. He had also dented Sooran's pride by escaping from his court, sowing enough doubt in Sooran's mind that he wasn't dealing with ordinary mortals anymore.

Senguntha ignited the battle in many ways that might mark Sooran's final confrontation.

SOORAN PREPARES FOR WAR

Senguntha received a hero's welcome upon his return to Senthilpuri. The warriors were ecstatic to see their commander back. Senguntha's lieutenants hugged him as he entered the main gate of Senthilpuri. Senguntha hastened to Muruga's quarters to meet his friend and Lord.

'Welcome back, my brother, how was your trip to Mahendrapuri?' asked a visibly elated Muruga, and embraced Senguntha.

'It was quite a journey, Muruga. Let me give you a summary,' said a weary Senguntha.

'I am eagerly awaiting to hear about your meeting with Sooran,' said Muruga gleefully.

'Sooran is consumed by his power. He didn't take you or your message seriously. He has categorically stated that he will not release the Suras at any cost. He threatened to decimate you and make the Suras his slaves forever,' summarized Senguntha.

'Let us grant him his wish, prepare for war!' declared Muruga to Senguntha and his lieutenants in a stern voice.

Senguntha and others bowed their heads in front of Muruga and left his quarters.

Senguntha went straight to Deva's quarters to pay his respects. He told Deva that he had met his son Jayanthan and reassured him that Muruga will soon put an end to his misery. An overwhelmed Deva hugged Senguntha.

Senguntha and Muruga were having dinner together after a long time.

'My dear friend, you didn't just walk into Sooran's court, did you? I am sure you would have had several escapades. Tell me about them,' said Muruga with a cheeky smile and wink.

'You know me inside out, I can't hide anything, can I?' said Senguntha, shaking his head side to side.

Senguntha narrated his entire journey to Mahendrapuri and back. He talked about the route, the grandeur of Mahendrapuri, and his rendezvous with Sooran. The minor battles he fought on the way killing several Asuras, including Sooran's son.

'Well, I told you to prepare for war, looks like you have already started it,' said Muruga and slapped his friend on his back.

Far away in Mahendrapuri, there was gloom and doom. Sooran had received the news about Vajrabahu's death. His body was brought before him. It was mutilated beyond recognition. Padmakomalai lay on the floor with dishevelled hair and screamed uncontrollably. She couldn't accept the untimely death of her young son. The man, who was *Chakravarthi,* broke down too. He couldn't bear the death of his son. Padmakomalai repeatedly blamed Sooran for her son's death. She was inconsolable.

Two days had passed since Vajrabahu's cremation, but Sooran was still in mourning. His minister Dharmakoban came to meet him in his private quarters.

'*Mannar Manna,* as a *Chakravarthi,* you cannot remain in this state of despair. The country, the clan, we all need you,' said Dharmakoban with hands held in namaskaram.

Sooran realized he had spent far too much time mourning his son. It was time for retribution.

'Dharmakoba, you are right; I had forgotten my duty as a king and a Kshatriya. Let us all assemble in the court tomorrow and discuss the next course of action,' said Sooran with authority.

Sooran hurriedly walked into his court and sat on his gigantic throne. The whole court stood up for the *Chakravarthi.* Sooran waved his hands and everyone took their seats. Sooran began to address the audience.

'Dear brethren, I burn with rage to obliterate every Sura, young or old in my sight. I want to eradicate their clan. However, it is our principle to discuss, debate, and plan our course of action, hence I have invited you all to the court,' Sooran said, still fuming with anger.

'We should have taken proactive measures when the boy and his army destroyed *Krauncha Malai* and Tharakan. If we had done so, we wouldn't have been in this situation. Let's pursue them and kill them all,' bellowed Mahishan, a senior minister in Sooran's cabinet.

One by one, every minister in the court, including the Chief Minister Dharmakoban, who had visited Sooran the previous night, spoke their minds. The common message that was rendered by one and all was to pursue proactively, Muruga and his army of upstarts and decimate them even before they set foot on Mahendrapuri.

'*Appa,* I don't know why you needed to call a meeting of all ministers and leaders of our clan for such a small matter. You didn't allow me to go, when uncle Tharakan was killed. I would have taken that boy captive, just as I captured Jayanthan. It's time to avenge Uncle Tharakan's and my little brother Vajrabahu's death. Place your trust in me; I won't fail you,' said Banukoban with conviction.

'*Anna,* I have been patiently listening to all that has been said so far,' said a booming voice from across the room.

It was Simhan.

He wanted to convey to his elder brother, his point of view.

'Speak up, Simhan, your views matter to me the most,' said Sooran.

'Everyone is talking emotionally and in a manner that would please you and not rationally. True advisers are the ones who explain the reality and provide a concrete course of action,' said a surprisingly calm Simhan.

'Stop talking in riddles and come to the point. Are you saying none of us here understand reality except you,' said Sooran, a little irked.

Anna, we have already brought down the Suras to their knees. We have punished them enough for the atrocities their forefathers committed on our clan. Life has now come full circle; it is now our turn. It is nothing but the cause-and-effect paradigm,' said Simhan philosophically.

'You are giving me spiritual sermons. Have you lost your mind? You are talking like a coward, not a Kshatriya,' fumed Sooran.

'I don't have any doubts about my valour, I am only stating the truth,' said Simhan calmly.

'Simha!' screamed Sooran as he stood up and removed his sword from his scabbard, but controlled himself and sat down on his throne again.

'Anger corrupts the mind, think calmly. It is in the best interest of our clan to release Jayanthan and other suras and hand them over to Muruga,' said Simhan, holding his hands in a *namaskaram*.

'Shame on you, Simha. We lost our brother and I have lost my son, yet you expect me to surrender,' screamed a livid Sooran.

'Muruga seems to be a divine child, blessed to achieve greatness. Perhaps it's the will of Lord Shiva,' said Simhan with a touch of reverence.

'Divine, my foot. Looks like you have been hallucinating lately. Age seems to have caught up with you and made you senile,' mocked Sooran.

'Mocking me will not change the reality in front of us. War should be the last resort and not the first,' said Simhan.

'If you are so scared of war, go to your palace and rest. I will let you know when we have decimated Muruga, his army, and killed every Sura; you can join the celebrations,' said Sooran and roared with laughter that echoed across the court.

Simhan knew that his brother had reached a point of no return. Anger, arrogance, and emotions were clouding his judgement, but Simhan was a warrior and it was his duty to protect his king and kingdom. He had a strong feeling that the end was near, so he decided to put himself on the line first.

'Pardon me, brother. Maybe I am overthinking. I will avenge our brother and my nephew. Let me lead the army and destroy everyone,' said Simhan with pride.

'Finally, you are talking like an Asura. Your words sound like music to my ears. Proud of you, my brother,' said Sooran and embraced Simhan.

Sooran got up from his throne, and the whole courtroom stood up.

Sooran passed a decree that Mahendrapuri was at war with Suras, Ganas, and everyone else who would take their side. He had the message sent to every nook and corner of the various kingdoms in the southern peninsula.

Mahendrapuri was now officially at war with the Suras and Ganas. Sooran instructed Simhan and Banukoban to oversee the war preparations. Sooran believed that it was his final battle that would obliterate the Suras from the earth forever.

BATTLE, BRAWN AND BLOOD

The sun shone brighter than usual at Senthilpuri. It was time for Muruga and his troops to embark on their journey to Mahendrapuri. Muruga instructed Senguntha to prepare his chariot, while Pawan eagerly awaited the opportunity to assist in the battle that would change the fate of the Suras forever. Senguntha had already convened all his key commanders and assembled the troops.

As the troops stood side by side, Muruga mounted his chariot and gave the signal to Pawan to drive the chariot beside the army that had assembled on the seashore. Pawan pulled the strings of the horses and the chariot sped like it was driven by the wind god himself. Every single soldier screamed the magic word '*Aro Hara!*' the word that bound everyone together with their commander.

As Muruga's chariot reached the edge of the ocean, it turned around. He stood up on the chariot and shouted '*Vetri Vel-Veera Vel.*' The entire regiment screamed in unison, and the beach shuddered as if there was an earthquake.

The army had built several boats based on the instructions provided by Deva and Vishwakarman since the day they had landed at Senthilpuri. Hundreds of small boats would transport them across the sea into Lanka Pattinam along with two huge cargo ships that would ferry the horses and elephants. It was the first time that the Ganas had seen naval architecture in play. It was an experience of a lifetime, and they were confident of their victory.

The long winding journey began with Senguntha captaining the lead ship that was showing the way to the rest of the cavalry. He was the only one who knew the way to Mahendrapuri. Deva was in the ship that brought up the rear of the gigantic army. As the ships and boats traversed the sea, it appeared as if a colossal dragon was weaving its way towards the land of Sooran, poised to unleash its fire and fury on the kingdom of the Asura *Chakravarthi* and reduce it to ashes.

Meanwhile, at Mahendrapuri, Sooran had a visitor. Sooran welcomed him with great fanfare and sought his blessings as he would soon be at War. It was Rishiraja, the great saint. Rishiraja forewarned Sooran that a legendary battle was about to unfold and that Muruga's name would be etched in the minds of people for eternity. He also cautioned Sooran that he wasn't fighting a battle with a young boy but an ultimate warrior, who was fulfilling his destiny. Sooran scoffed at Rishiraja's words.

'Maharishi, the very reason he is still alive is because I thought he was a young boy. Now that you mention that he is a warrior, its time I taught him a lesson,' said Sooran with disdain.

Meanwhile, Muruga's army had started to arrive at Lanka Pattinam in large numbers. They marched through the deserted city and reached the northern part of Mahendrapuri. Muruga had instructed Vishwakarman to establish a *paasarai, a barrack.* The work had started in earnest, and within two weeks, the entire army, with its personnel and arsenal were placed in the barrack at the northern front. The name given to the *paasarai* was Hemakootam, in other words The Golden Gathering.

According to the principles of war followed in those times, armies would only engage in battle once the commanders on either side announced it. This was done by blowing the conch or the bugle to signal the start of the war. It was a time when dharmic values governed all the clans.

Sooran's spies who were watching the activities unfolding at Lanka Pattinam decided it was time to inform their king that the enemy was battle-ready and that the Asuras could declare war.

'Lord, our spy Goran is here to see u,' said a soldier to Sooran, who waved his hand to bring him in.

'Greetings to the *Chakravathi*. Muruga's army has set up a barrack on the northern part of Mahendrapuri near Lanka Pattinam. He has a huge army with him,' said Goran.

'Finally, the baby elephant has come to the lion's den,' said Sooran and let out a huge roar of laughter.

Sooran sent word through his guards to bring his son, Banukoban, to the court. Banukoban immediately left his palace to see his father.

'*Appa,* you wanted to see me?' asked Banukoban with folded hands.

'*Kumaara,* the day you've been waiting for has finally arrived,' said Sooran addressing Banukoban fondly as his beloved son.

'Muruga and his entourage are stationed at the northern part of our kingdom. Go and vanquish them and avenge your brother's and uncle's deaths,' said Sooran, with anger and anguish written all over his face.

'It is my duty, I will make the young man flee, and I will capture his army. We will release them only if Swayambhu seeks your pardon,' said Banukoban proudly.

'May Lord Rudra be with you. *Jayam* will be yours,' said Sooran, patting his son on his back and wishing him victory in battle.

Banukoban left the court in a hurry and went straight to his quarters. He paid his obeisance to Veeralakshmi, the goddess of valour. He then took his mother's blessings and went to the Armoury to inspect the weapons. He called his commanders and asked them to be prepared to leave at dawn.

At the stroke of dawn, Banukoban left his palace with a massive army consisting of horses, elephants, chariots, and foot soldiers. They shook the earth with their march as they reached the northern frontier and set up their camp. A soldier rushed into Muruga's quarters, where he and Senguntha were in conversation. He told them that the Asura army had arrived with Banukoban at its helm.

'Senguntha, lead our Army to war with Banukoban and his Asura warriors. Come back victorious,' said Muruga hugging his commander.

Senguntha's and Banukoban' s army were now face to face with each other. Senguntha took out his white conch and blew it to indicate that they were ready for war. Banukoban took a bugle and sounded it in reply, signalling that they were ready too.

Both commanders raised their swords from their scabbards, pointed them towards the enemy, and screamed, 'Attack!' The entire army on both sides sped towards each other. It was like two massive tsunami waves colliding with tremendous force. Within seconds the swords clashed with one another, creating huge metallic sounds that filled the air.

The ferocity with which Muruga's army fought took the Asura army by surprise, but they too fought with great valour. Hands were mutilated, blood spurted out from warriors, and heads rolled. It was a brutal blood bath.

It was now clear that the Asura army was on the defensive. Banukoban sensed his army weakening. He called out to his lieutenant, Anali to go and attack Senguntha's army. Anali drove his chariot into the war front and plucked his bow, the sound reverberating through the warring clans, who stood still for a moment.

Senguntha asked his lieutenant, Singar to fight Anali. Anali sent multiple arrows at Singar who repelled them with arrows of his own. Before Anali could let the next set of arrows fly, Singar shot down the horses driving Anali's chariot. Singar then jumped on to Anali's chariot and broke his bow with bare hands. An enraged Anali picked up a spear to hit Singar on the head, but Singar blocked it with his left hand and kicked Anali in his chest, causing him to fall from his seat. Singar wasn't done; he picked Anali up, rotated him in the air, and threw him down on the ground. As Anali hit the ground, his skull broke and he died instantly.

With Anali dead, it was the Ajamugan's turn to step forward to fight Singar. Like a tag team championship, Singar stepped back, and Madhu from Senguntha's army stepped forward to fight Ajamugan.

Ajamugan took aim at Madhu and was about to release a set of arrows when Madhu threw his mace at him, breaking the bow into pieces.

'It is against dharmic principles to fight a warrior without weapons; hence, I pardon you,' said Madhu.

Ajamugan, an Asura, would rather die than be pardoned by an enemy warrior. He took out the wheel of his chariot and hurled it at the retreating Madhu, who was forewarned by Singar. Madhu avoided being hit by the chariot wheel. He quickly swirled, took a spear from his chariot and hurled it on to Ajamugan. It pierced through him and got stuck in the ground. The force lifted Ajamugan off his feet, leaving his dead body dangling from the spear stuck in the ground.

Banukoban had seen enough. Banukoban decided it was time to enter the battlefield. He roared onto the battlefield in his chariot, sending arrows at will in all directions and killing every Gana warrior in sight. The entire frontline of the Ganas were destroyed.

Senguntha's brother, Veerakesari, stepped forward and accosted Banukoban.

'Banukoba, if you are a true warrior, fight one-on-one with me and not kill ordinary soldiers,' bellowed Veerakesari.

'Who are you to teach me about the principles of war? I am the Crown Prince of Mahendrapuri. I will, however, grant you the honour; prepare to die,' screamed Banukoban, raising his bow in the air.

The two warriors started to strike each other with arrows. Every arrow Banukoban sent was countered by Veerakesari. Banukoban decided to change tack and fight with a spear. He got down from his chariot, and so did Veerakesari. A severe fight ensued between the two, with sparks flying when the spears clashed with each other. Neither was able to break down the other. Banukoban threw down the spear, took his sword, and invited Veerakesari to pick up a sword as well. The sharpness of the metal blades created fire and smoke as they clashed. It went on for quite some time, but no victor emerged. Banukoban decided it was time to use his trickery. He brought out his sorcery and created an illusion of multiple Banukoban's in front of Veerakesari. When Veerakesari got distracted by the sorcery, he attacked him from behind and slit his throat. A valiant Veerakesari fell to the ground, face down.

News of Veerakesari's death reached Senguntha, and he decided to step into the battlefield. He knew that the status of the war had changed after Banukoban's direct entry to the war zone. He couldn't be defeated just by courage and valour.

Senguntha's chariot came in front of Banukoban's chariot. On seeing Senguntha, Banukoban roared in laughter.

'Looks like the boy ran away and sent his messenger to fight me instead. You wouldn't be alive today if my father had sent me instead of my little brother,' said Banukoban with utter disdain.

'A true warrior doesn't keep talking about his greatness; he shows that in his actions. Stop the lecture and fight me if you can,' said Senguntha with a smirk.

An enraged Banukoban sent a flurry of arrows towards Senguntha, who countered them with ease. The sequence continued for some more time. It looked as if the army on both sides decided to stop fighting for a while and watch the two great warriors fight a pitch battle. Banukoban used every weapon he had it as disposal, and everything was swatted away effortlessly by Senguntha. After all, he had learnt the art of war from the great Swayambhu. Banukoban decided to use sorcery again.

He invoked *mogasthram, a weapon that would create acid fumes.* He sent the arrows in all direction like tear gas shells, and the Gana army fell unconscious because of the acid fumes, including the great Senguntha. Before Banukoban could attack an unarmed Senguntha, the heavens opened up. It seemed as though Lord *Varuna,* the rain god, wanted to support Muruga in this war to re- establish Dharma. There was lightning and thunder in the sky, and torrential rain poured down, neutralizing the acid fumes created by Banukoban.

Senguntha got up choking. He had seen enough and wanted to end the battle with Banukoban here and now. He strung his bow with an arrow in the shape of *thirisoolam*. It was an arrow gifted to him by Swayambhu before he left for the battle. It resembled the trident of Lord Shiva. The only counter to the arrow was another trident arrow. Although Banukoban possessed the same, he didn't have it with him as he had underestimated the enemy. He knew he had to surrender and live to fight another day. Banukoban dropped his weapons and folded his hands in prayer. Senguntha brought his bow down, understanding that the enemy didn't wish to fight. Banukoban retreated, and with him the Asura warriors.

The Sun was also slowly descending into the horizon. As dusk approached, Senguntha blew his conch to signal the end of the first day of the war.

SOORAN ENTERS THE WARZONE

Sooran could not sleep at night. The Asura clan's pride had been severely dented when his son ran away from the battle and conceded defeat. It was another matter that Banukoban wanted to live to fight another day as he had the *thirisoolam* arrow with him. Unfortunately, he had underestimated his enemy and had not come fully prepared.

Sooran commanded all the clans now under his authority to join the war. He sent word through spies to the respective kingdoms to assemble in Mahendrapuri in the shortest possible time. Meanwhile, Sooran himself decided to lead his army into the battlefield. Banukoban sulked in anger but had no choice but to accept his father's command, after all, he was the *Chakravarthi.*

Sooran asked his nephews to join him in the war the next day. He was joined by Adhisooran, Simhan's son, and Indiran, who was waiting to avenge his father Tharakan's death. They thanked Sooran for giving them the opportunity to fight in the prestigious battle aimed at restoring Asura supremacy. Following their war tradition, the king and princes prayed to goddess Veera Lakshmi before they set out for battle.

The Asura cavalry arrived slightly earlier than usual. It was Deva's turn to check if the enemy was ready for battle. He noticed a huge army led by three commanders. He could clearly make out from the chariot and the sounds made by the Asura warriors that it was none other than Sooran who had come to the warzone. He panicked and ran towards Muruga.

'The moment we have all been waiting for has arrived. Sooran has entered the battlefield. It's time for you to come,' said Deva with humility.

'*Yaam Irukka Bayam Yen,*' Muruga said nonchalantly.

Muruga called upon his troops to follow him. Pawan brought the chariot instantly in front of Muruga, who boarded it and raised his *Vel* and the entire army screamed in unison, '*Vetri Vel -Veera Vel.*' Muruga led the army to the front to face the dreaded Sooran. However, Sooran wasn't ready to oblige just yet. The king of kings wouldn't battle a young boy. He asked Adhisooran to go ahead and challenge Muruga in battle. Sooran sounded the bugle, and Muruga sounded the Conch to signal the beginning of the day's battle.

Muruga, on his part, decided to play mind games with Sooran. He sent out Uggiran, one of the trusted lieutenants of Swayambhu, to fight Adhisooran.

The two mighty warriors stood face-to-face in their respective chariots. Adhisooran rained arrows at Uggiran, who countered them with his own set of arrows. They nullified each other. Uggiran threw his spear to break the wheel of Adhisooran's chariot. Adhisooran jumped in time to avoid getting crushed. The force was so great that the horses succumbed to the weight of the chariot. Adhisooran decided to use sorcery in his next move. He sent a flurry of arrows with fire on their tips. It was as though Agni, the lord of fire, had come to war. Uggiran jumped out of his chariot, which was burnt to ashes. Uggiran prayed to Muruga for saving his life as he believed that Muruga was Swayambhu himself. Before Adhisooran could make his next move, Uggiran threw a spear that broke Adhisooran's armour. Adhisooran had to go for the kill, he picked up his spear to ram it into Uggiran's chest, but Uggiran was too quick for him. He grabbed the spear, turned it around and rammed it into Adhisooran's throat, bringing him a bloody death.

It was now Indiran's turn to step in. He unleashed a flurry of arrows, killing many Gana soldiers instantly. Kanagan, a leader from the Gana army stepped forward to fight Indiran. He fought valiantly with Indiran, but the speed and accuracy of Indiran's arrows were so great that he couldn't keep up and eventually succumbed to them.

After Kanagan died, Unmatthan stepped forward to battle Indiran. He too waged a valiant battle but alas he was no match for the strength of Indiran and he too succumbed. Following Unmatthan, Manthan tried to stop the losses of Muruga's army, but he was up against a formidable foe who was fighting like a man possessed. Indiran was not only fighting for Sooran but also seeking revenge for his father's death. At one point, Manthan raised his hand in defeat, and Indiran let him go.

Senguntha knew it was time to step in and finish this battle. He confronted Indiran and challenged him. A bloody battle ensued between the two of them. Each pierced the other's armour with a flurry of arrows, and they were now battling with their swords, cutting each other stroke by stroke. The battle continued for a while. When Senguntha sensed his opponent was tiring, he used every ounce of strength within him for one final assault and cut off Indiran's right hand. A stunned and bleeding Indiran tried to fight Senguntha by throwing a spear at him with his weaker hand, but it just grazed Senguntha's head gear. Severe loss of blood made Indiran feel dizzy and unbalanced. Siezing the moment, with a swift stroke of his sword, Senguntha severed Indiran's head bringing a bloody end to the battle.

Sooran watched the demise of both his nephews from a distance and was simultaneously livid with anger and shell-shocked by the outcome. He ordered his charioteer to take him to the main war front. Once he arrived, he pulled the strings of his bow. The sound reverberated across the battlefield like a thousand thunders striking at the same time. The warriors were stunned and stopped fighting.

Senguntha, who was watching the events unfolding in front of him, stood with his three cousins, Veera Marthandan, Veera Rakshadhan, and Veera Senan. He called upon Veera Marthandan to challenge Sooran. Veera Marthandan stepped forward to fight Sooran and sent a flurry of arrows towards Sooran, but Sooran swatted them away like flies. Sooran then unleashed an arrow, which struck Veera Marthandan in the chest and burst through to the other side, causing instant death. This sent shivers down the spines of the Gana and Sura warriors.

Veera Rakshadhan, who was beside Senguntha, sought his permission to fight Sooran. Senguntha nodded, and Veera Rakshadhan jumped into the fray to fight Sooran. Veera Rakshadan let loose a dozen arrows towards Sooran, who replied with one arrow that ripped through the dozen arrows and hit Veera Rakshadan's headgear. Before he could react, Sooran sent a flurry of arrows that destroyed Veera Rakshadan's entire chariot. An enraged Veera Rakshadhan ran towards Sooran with his gigantic Sword and struck Sooran's bow, but the sword broke into pieces. Sooran caught hold of Veera Rakshadan by his neck and flung him into the air. He fell with a huge thud that broke his skull and ribs, leaving him immobile on the ground. Sooran spat in the direction where the paralyzed Veera Rakshadhan lay. Sooran didn't want to waste his energy on a man who was paralyzed for life.

Veera Senan, the last of Senguntha's cousins, now stepped forward to challenge Sooran. He sent a flurry of arrows towards Sooran, who swatted them away with ease, like small toys. Sooran unleased a flurry of arrows which brought down his opponent's chariot. Veera Senan jumped out and ran towards Sooran. Sooran released an arrow at the approaching Veera Senan that removed his head gear. The next arrow pierced his shoulder, and a third hit is abdomen. A bleeding Veera Senan ran towards Sooran in an attempt to somehow kill with his sword. Sooran let out a roar of laughter and jumped out from his chariot. He picked up Veera Senan like a wrestler, swirled him around and threw him into the air. Veera Senan landed with such force that his neck snapped and blood started gushing out of his mouth; it was a gory death.

Senguntha witnessed the killing of all his cousins and was astounded by the strength, power, and prowess of Sooran. It was now his turn to face the Asura King, who was waiting for more blood to quench his thirst. He now saw the messenger who had killed his son standing before him.

'You murdered my son. Your agonizing death will serve as a warning to anyone who dares to harm any Asura,' said Sooran, now red faced with rage.

'I am a servant of Lord Muruga. I would play the role of a messenger or a mercenary as my lord wishes. Now I am the mercenary,' said Senguntha calmly.

Sooran, now a raging inferno, sent out a flurry of arrows. Senguntha countered them with his own. Senguntha invoked Lord Yama through the mantra taught by Swayambhu and sent an arrow towards Sooran. The arrow fell down as if it had it a giant mountain. A stunned Senguntha then took out the *thirisoolam* arrow and shot it towards Sooran, who in turn released his own *thirisoolam* arrow. The arrows nullified each other. Senguntha had no more powerful weapons left. He prayed to Lord Shiva and threw a spear at Sooran. The spear, on hitting Sooran's body armour, broke into pieces. Senguntha knew his game was over. Sooran threw his spear in a flash at Senguntha, striking his chest and causing profuse bleeding. Visali, Senguntha's charioteer, immediately turned the chariot around and led Senguntha out of the battle zone.

'Senguntha is no more!' screamed the Asura warriors. '*Asureswaran Vaazhga Vaazhga*,' reverberated in the battlefield. The Gana warriors and the Suras were stunned upon hearing the news and were losing morale. Sensing this, the Asura warriors mounted an aggressive attack on Muruga's army. It was time for the anointed one to step into the warzone. Muruga asked Pawan to take his chariot to the lead position in front of Sooran. Pawan obliged, and the two adversaries were face to face for the first time.

Looking at Muruga, Sooran wondered. At such a young age, this boy is fearless and dares to face me in battle. Although his bête noire stood before him, Sooran felt a sense of compassion towards Muruga. The thought soon changed, and Sooran started to address Muruga.

'Muruga, your father is the most revered by us. He has given us his word that he would never wage a battle against us,' said Sooran in a surprisingly calm demeanour.

'Hey Asureswara, that's precisely why I sent a messenger to inform you about our request. Alas, you chose to reject it,' said Muruga like a preacher.

'The Suras have brain washed you into believing that we have been unjust while they have been fair, which is far from the truth,' argued Sooran.

'I am not fighting for the Suras, I am fighting to restore Dharma,' said Muruga nonchalantly.

'You have seen my power. Do you still wish to fight me? You have so much life ahead of you,' said a compassionate Sooran.

'I am in the battlefield in front of you. Does that not tell you, my choice?' said Muruga with a smirk.

'I am the King of Kings. I have great power bestowed upon me by Lord Shiva, I have every clan under my thumb,' roared Sooran.

'More than you, it is your 'I' that is going to lead you to your downfall,' said Muruga with composure.

'You little brat, you have decided to die an untimely death. I pity Swayambhu,' exclaimed Sooran with disdain, stringing his arrow.

Sooran let loose a flurry of arrows at Muruga, who matched them with his own set of arrows. Before Sooran could come up with the next set of arrows, Muruga shot down the flag on Sooran's chariot. With his pride hurt, Sooran decided to up the ante and sent out more arrows imbued with tantrik powers, and Muruga shot them down with ease. Now it was all or nothing for Sooran. He took out the *Nagasthram* and shot it towards Muruga. Muruga knew there was no counter to this weapon. He dropped his weapon and prayed to Lord Shiva with folded hands. The arrow whizzed past him, taking his crown with it. Muruga knew his prayers had been answered. He lifted a spear and thew it on Sooran, it broke his armour. Before Sooran could react, Muruga unleashed a flurry of arrows, bringing down his chariot. Muruga jumped out of his chariot, ran towards Sooran and raised his Shakthi *Vel*, which shone like a thousand suns, to ram it into Sooran's throat. Sooran was now bereft of weapons, armour, and a chariot.

'Soora, it is against principles of a Dharmic war to hurt someone who is standing as a *nirayuthapani, weaponless.* There is still time. Mull over my offer and come back tomorrow if you still wish to fight,' said Muruga in a sombre tone.

Absolutely devastated by what had just happened, Sooran was lost in thought. It seemed for a moment that the earth stood still. He couldn't, in his wildest dreams envisage something like this happening to him. He thought he would never lose a battle to anyone, let alone a young upstart in his first battle. He hung his head in shame, turned around and left in a huff. Muruga raised his hands, and everyone gave way to the king of kings, who was walking back with his head down. His pride had been smashed but not his will to fight.

REDEMPTION & RESURRECTION

Two days had passed, since his humiliation at the hands of Muruga. Late into the night, Sooran wrestled with sleeplessness. His mind was consumed by the events that had happened couple of days ago. He was humiliated in battle by a young boy. Was it really the end of his reign or was there some hope? As he was lost in thought, he saw his son Banukoban enter the room.

'*Appa*, I came to check on you as you have been silent for the past two days,' said Banukoba with curiosity.

Silence prevailed as Sooran was still lost in thought.

'I am eager to know about the status of the war as you didn't allow me to come with you to the battlefield. Give me a chance again and I shall prove my mettle,' said Banukoban with conviction.

Sooran came out of his bubble and looked at Banukoban as if he was seeing him for the first time.

'I almost got the better of that bloody warrior turned messenger Senguntha. If only I had been more prepared,' lamented Banukoban.

Sooran saw the determination and the frustration in his son and decided it was time to tell him about the state of the war.

'I am glad that you want to confront Muruga and Senguntha but winning this battle needs more than mere valour,' said Sooran soberly.

'Let me to go to the war tomorrow. I will slay Senguntha and bring Muruga to you as a captive, you decide his fate,' said Banukoban in anger.

Sooran was overwhelmed with emotion upon seeing the courage and gumption of his son, the crown prince of Mahendrapuri. He hugged Banukoban and patted him on the back.

'Banukoba, Muruga is no ordinary mortal. It is not possible for you to fight him and win but you take on Senguntha, while I challenge Muruga to battle,' said Sooran, wiping out a few tear drops from his eyes.

'I will return only if I avenge my brother's death by butchering that bloody messenger,' said Banukoban seething with rage.

'It's time to entrust you with a family heirloom, my son,' said Sooran as he led Banukoban towards the armoury.

Father and son reached the armoury, which was packed with weapons of all shapes and sizes. Sooran turned to an old picture on the wall. It was the picture of his mother, Maya. He removed the painting from the wall. Behind the painting was a hidden knob. When he twisted the knob, a brick opened below it, revealing a secret draw within it. Sooran reached into the crevice and pulled out an arrow, it was glittering like gold and had the inscription *Maya* on it.

'Banukoba, here is a gift from your grandmother, chant her name on your lips and make a wish before sending this arrow towards your enemy and your wish will be granted,' said Sooran as he handed it over to his son.

'You have my blessings and your grandmother's weapon. Nothing can stop you now!' said Sooran hugging his son.

'Senguntha, here I come,' roared Banukoban.

Meanwhile at Hemakootam, Muruga and Senguntha were having a quiet dinner.

'Senguntha, I expect Banukoban to return tomorrow and challenge you for a fight. Be ready for your battle with him. He is a shrewd and cunning warrior, who uses both weapons and sorcery,' said Muruga.

'You are my greatest weapon. When you are with me, I fear no one,' replied Senguntha proudly.

The next day marked a new dawn for both Banukoban and Senguntha. The two commanders led their armies to the northern part of Mahendrapuri.

Banukoban sent a soldier across with a palm-leaf manuscript that had a message meant only for Senguntha. The Asura soldier delivered the message with reverence.

'Greetings Commander, this message is from our leader specifically addressed to you,' said the soldier.

Senguntha looked at the folded palm leaf and opened it to read its content.

'Till Death– You and I" it read.

'Tell your commander, I am ready and ask him to say his prayers as well,' retorted Senguntha to the soldier.

Both the armies stood still. It was round two of the battle between Senguntha and Banukoban. The previous round was won by Senguntha as Banukoban left the battle field. This time however, he was fully prepared. Senguntha on the other hand was under no illusion that this would be an easy battle. He had already been forewarned by Muruga.

The two warriors sounded their conch and bugle respectively to start the battle.

Banukoba pulled the string of his arrow and it thundered, a reciprocal thunder was witnessed from the other end. Banukoban let go a dozen arrows towards Senguntha who replied with his own set of arrows. Banukoban decided to move his chariot in a circle, while he continued to fire arrows. Senguntha directed his charioteer to do the same. A dust storm was created as the chariots swerved and swiveled, while the two warriors let go of their fearsome arrows, the battle raged for a while but they kept nullifying each other. Banukoban had seen enough. He decided to use the *Shivastram,* ordinary weapons were of no use. Senguntha also had the *Shivastram* that was gifted to him by Swayambhu.

Both the armies ran helter-skelter as both warriors strung their respective arrows. This was the most potent weapon present at that point in time and would create great destruction to the entire place. Not only the warriors, everything around them would be reduced to ashes. This was only meant to be a deterrent and never to be used offensively. Banukoban wanted to win at all cost, he let go of the *Shivastram* and so did Senguntha. There was a massive explosion in mid-air as the two arrows collided with a deafening sound. A mushroom cloud emerged, and smoke engulfed both the armies. There was acid rain pouring from the sky, destroying everything as it hit the ground. Several soldiers of both armies bore the brunt of the weapon. Mutilated bodies were lying across the battlefield, charred beyond recognition, with smoke still emanating from some of them. It looked like the day of the Apocalypse. Muruga and Sooran were apprised about the use of *Shivastram* by the warriors and there had been severe causalities on both sides.

The battle was still not over. Banukoban knew, his grandmothers' weapon was still with him and the time had come to use it. He had failed with the *Mogasthra,* he was not going to fail with *Mayasthra.* He didn't wish instant death for Senguntha; He wanted to see Muruga and others suffer. Hence, he decided that he would cast a spell that would put Senguntha into a coma. He would be alive but dead for all practical purposes. This was a better revenge than just killing him instantly. He took out the weapon, invoked his grandmother in his mind, and wished that Senguntha should fall into a coma, then let go of the arrow. Senguntha realized something untoward was going to happen. Before he could decide on a counter measure, the arrow hit him on his chest and within seconds Senguntha lost consciousness and his unconscious body rolled out from his chariot on to the ground.

Banukoban let out a cry of triumph and the Asuras joined in, 'Setthaan Sengunthan', *Senguntha is dead.* The Gana army was too stunned to react; they didn't know what to do. One of the soldiers rode back to inform Muruga about the great misery that had befallen them. Banukoban sounded the bugle to end the day's proceedings as the commander of the enemy was now slain. The war was moving towards a decisive end.

The city of Mahendrapuri was decorated like never before. *Thoranam's and Maalai's* were all over town. There were firecrackers across the city. People were dancing and singing praises of Sooran and Banukoban. As Banukoban walked through the outer gate, people showered petals on him as chants of *'yuvarjar vaazhga', 'thalapathi vaazhga'* rendered the air. The people were wishing their crown prince and commander with long life.

An elated Padmakomalai welcomed her eldest son. She kept a *thilakam, a red vermillion mark* on his forehead indicating a victory welcome. Banukoban fell at her feet. She lifted him and planted a peck on his cheek. It was a proud moment for Padmakomalai, as her eldest son had vanquished the enemy and avenged the death of his brother.

Sooran awaited his son in the courtroom along with his brother Simhan and his council of ministers. A beaming Banukoban entered the courtroom. He was greeted with *'yuvarajar vaazhga', 'thalapathi vaazhga',* yet again. Banukoban accepted the wishes of all present with folded hands as he took his throne.

Sooran addressed the gathering and said, 'This is a very proud day for me and my family. My son has come of age. Behold your future king,' and lifted Banukoban's hand in the air. Everyone threw the rose petals they had in their hands onto Banukoban and blessed him.

Far away at Hemakootam there was an eerie silence as Senguntha's lifeless body was placed at the centre of all the barracks. The soldiers were inconsolable. Deva, Muruga, and Pawan were all sitting around the pedestal on which Senguntha was kept.

Muruga was still unfazed with what had unfolded during the day.

'Muruga, how are you not moved by the situation? He was your dear friend,' said Deva with tears flowing down his cheeks.

'Deva, you have given up hope, I haven't. You are looking at the problem; I am looking for the solution,' said Muruga in a calm demeanour.

Deva was perplexed by the statement but didn't know how to react, although Muruga was right in some way. Senguntha was in coma and not dead.

'Every spell has an antidote just like we have antidotes for poison. Let's talk to Dhanvantri.'

Dhanvantari was the royal physician of the Suras.

'Greetings, Muruga. You called for me,' asked Dhanvantri, with hands folded in *namaskaram*.

'What is the method to break the spell on Senguntha? We can't leave him like this and continue the war,' said Muruga.

'Muruga, Sanjivani is the only remedy that will get Senguntha out of this spell. We don't know where it grows and how to get it,' said Dhanvantri with a tremble in his voice.

Muruga thought for a moment and then had a smile on his face. It was as though an idea flashed in his mind.

'Hanuman had got Sanjivani for Lakshman here in Lanka and he travelled across this very sea. What if the fragments of Sanjeevini had fallen here? maybe we just need to look for it,' declared Muruga.

'Pardon me, my Lord, that war happened several thousand years ago. How would we ever get Sanjivani now,' said Dhanvantri with a quizzical look on his face.

'The sun has existed for several thousand years. Countless organisms still exist after thousands of years.

Humanity itself has endured several millennia, so why not Sanjivani?' asked Muruga.

It was impossible to beat Muruga in argument and logic as he always had a counter.

Muruga called Pawan, Deva, and Varun and instructed them to look for Sanjivani in the small floating islands nearby. The search party began in the night and by noon the next day, Pawan chanced upon an island which had a great herbal smell on it. He sent out a flare from the island which indicated he had found something. Deva and

Dhanvantri took a boat and reached the island. To everyone's dismay, Dhanvantri took a blade of grass in his hand and said, 'Sanjivani.' The word Sanjivini meant 'giver of life.' It could once again save another brave warrior.

They rushed back with bags full of the magical herb. The herb was boiled and Dhanvantri took a jar full of the concoction. Muruga took Senguntha and put him on his lap they covered the face and Dhanvantri let the fumes engulf Senguntha's nose and head. Within few minutes, Senguntha gasped for air. He was still in a dizzy state but the medicine had worked. Senguntha was out of coma but still weak as the organs still needed to get to their full functioning.

Dhanvantri fell at Muruga's feet, who lifted him up.

'With hands folded in a prayer position, Dhanvantri said, 'Muruga, you are truly blessed by the divine!'

Senguntha recuperated in a special tent tended by nurses through day and night, He was expected to fully recover in a few days.

Two days after the miraculous recovery of Senguntha, Deva and Muruga were taking an evening stroll around Hemakootam.

'Muruga, how did you come to the point of view that there could be Sanjivani nearby,' asked Deva.

'Deva, our ancestors across India were extraordinary people, who had knowledge, wisdom, and courage in abundance. All our ancient scriptures describe the truth, we call it *ithihasam, history as it happened.* We need to trust our ancestors and their ability and not just read the ancient scriptures like stories. We tend to believe what we see; it is not the mistake of our ancestors that we can't see their greatness. It shows that we are myopic,' concluded Muruga.

Far away at Mahendrapuri, the victory party was still on. The revelry of the Asuras was well known. They fought hard and partied harder. Sooran and his warriors believed they had broken the spine of their enemy by eliminating Senguntha, oblivious of what was happening at Hemakootam. The scales were tilting back to equilibrium. The war was becoming like a game of chess, with every move having a counter move.

Muruga awaited Sooran's next move.

SOORAN IN DISTRESS

Amidst the great revelry in Mahendrapuri, a soldier walked into Sooran's palace, and in a hushed tone conversed with a senior minister in Sooran's cabinet. The minister's expression changed, and he dismissed the soldier.

After all the din settled down, the minister conveyed to Soora the rather unfortunate news of Senguntha's revival by Dhanvantri using Muruga's wisdom. Sooran couldn't believe his ears; he wondered if Muruga was actually human. Muruga's vision and skills surpassed his age, keeping him one step ahead of Sooran in this war.

A contemplative Sooran sat on his bed, wondering whether he would be able to win this war at all. Just then, he heard a voice calling out to him. It was his younger son, Hiranyan.

'Appa, I know the war is bothering you endlessly,' said a young Hiranyan.

'You are too young to worry about my troubles,' said Sooran with a sarcastic smile.

'I want to ask you something. Am I old enough for that?' asked Hiranyan sarcastically, with palms folded in a *namaskaram*.

'Go ahead!' Sooran said, pointing his palm towards Hiranyan.

'You are a great devotee of Lord Shiva. You have practiced tantra, praying to Goddess Kali. You were considered invincible. Why is there a sudden change in your fortune?' asked Hiranyan with all humility.

'You are mistaken; there is no change in my fortune. Battles take a long time; sometimes you have to lose battles to win a war,' retorted Sooran.

'Maybe it's a sign that you have overstepped your line and delved too much into Adharma, that Lord Rudra decided to restore balance,' prophesized Hiranyan.

'Utter nonsense!'

'I don't know who teaches you such foolish things they should be hanged,' said Sooran angrily.

'You continue to harass the Suras. Jayanthan is still captive along with the other Suras, even though they have accepted you as *Chakravarthi*. It doesn't seem right, does it?' said Hiranyan.

'Hiranya, you have crossed your limits. I never knew my son would turn out to be a coward. Get lost! screamed Sooran.

'My apologies if I have crossed my limits. As your son, I was only sharing my point of view. I am also duty-bound to protect my king and kingdom, which I shall do.'

'I will take my leave,' said Hiranyan, folding his hands in *namaskaram*, bowing to Sooran.

Sooran was enraged by the conversation with his son. However, it had sown the seed of confusion and self- doubt in his mind. *'Is Hiranyan actually right?'* he wondered.

The next morning, Hiranyan appeared in Sooran's private quarters, fully armoured. He bowed down and sought his blessings. Hiranyan's decision to wage battle against Muruga's army brought joy to Sooran, who hugged him.

'I am proud of you, my son. A true Kshatriya shows his thoughts in actions, not in mere talk of wisdom. Victory will be yours! Lord Rudra is with you,' said Sooran, beaming.

Hiranyan departed with Sooran's army to the northern front to confront Muruga and the Gana Army. It was his first experience with war. He was determined to do something for his disgruntled father. If he lived to share his victory, his father would feel proud. If he died in battle, he would achieve the honour of a Kshatriya and be seen as a martyr by his father and the Asuras. It was a risk worth taking.

Hiranyan blew his conch to signal the beginning of the day's battle. He didn't know who he would face. A chariot raced towards him from the opponent's camp and stopped in front of him. The warrior introduced himself as Neelan, appointed by Senguntha to challenge Hiranyan in battle.

Hiranyan picked up a spear and hurled it at Neelan, who protected himself with a shield and hurled his spear towards the wheel of Hiranyan's chariot. The wheel broke causing an imbalance to the chariot. In the nick of time, Hiranyan leaped out. He now drew arrows from his quiver and fired them at Neelan, who replied with his own set of arrows. Hiranyan realized that he was not going to win this battle by fighting with weapons alone, so just like every other Asura, he turned to sorcery. He disappeared from the scene. While Neelan was looking for him, he appeared behind him and struck him with an arrow; a bleeding Neelan fell down.

As he lifted his bow to fire an arrow into the back of the wounded Neelan, a sharp arrow struck his bow from behind and broke it instantly. A startled Hiranyan turned around and was dismayed to see Senguntha seated on his chariot; he couldn't believe his eyes.

'A true Kshatriya doesn't kill his enemy from behind. Be brave and fight face to face with me,' said Senguntha.

Hiranyan had neither the nuance, nor the weapons to fight Senguntha. He bowed to Senguntha and left the battlefield.

Ashamed of his inability to fight for his country, he chose not to return to Mahendrapuri. He departed the frontier, took a boat to an uninhabited island, and vowed never to return. As he sailed, he felt the Asura clan's end was near. He also figured out the answers to the questions that he had posed to his father earlier. He believed his only contribution would be to perform the final rites for his father and brothers when the time came.

Gana warriors raised victory slogans while Asura warriors retreated as their commander had fled. News reached the *Chakravarthi* that his son had fled the battlefield. An incensed Sooran felt angered and embarrassed. He wanted to find and kill his son with his bare hands for cowardice. At the same time, he felt ashamed for not leading the battle himself and for sending a small boy to face the wrath of Muruga's army.

A confused Sooran was walking up and down his private chamber with his mind filled with anger and guilt, pondering his next move. He was so lost in thought that he didn't notice his son Agnimugan come into the room. Having heard the news about Hiranyan, he came to comfort his father.

'*Appa*, it hurts to see the *Chakravarthi* in a state of despair,' said Agnimugan with a genuine concern for his father.

'My son, I seem to be fighting a losing battle. I have lost my nephews. I have been humiliated in battle by a young boy, and now I foolishly sent Hiranyan, knowing he was incapable, and he has humiliated me further. I am bereft of strategic thinking to win this war.' said Sooran in anguish.

'*Appa*, I am still here and are so are Banukoban and Uncle Simhan. Be rest assured, we will win this war,' said Agnimugan, instilling confidence in Sooran.

An overwhelmed Sooran hugged his son. Agnimugan had provided a sense of belief that the Asuras could still win the war. Sooran's head believed that the enemy had the upper hand, but his heart believed that the tide would turn. He blessed Agnimugan and wished him victory in tomorrow's battle.

Meanwhile, at Hemakootam, Deva was having a conversation with Muruga and Senguntha, who had now fully recovered.

'This is a war of attrition for both sides, and we still aren't anywhere close to finishing it,' said a worried Deva.

'Old habits die hard, they say. Have you started to question my ability again' chided Muruga.

'Not at all. You are our only hope, but every drop of Asura blood seems to create a new enemy daily,' said Deva.

'This war is a *Chakravyuh*. The closer we get to the core, the harder the battle. In war and in life, the greater the goal, greater is the effort in achieving it,' philosophized Muruga.

'I agree, Muruga. Even Bhagwan Krishna had to climb up on his friends to get the prized possession in Gokul. We are mere mortals. However, once the pinnacle is reached, all the effort seems worthwhile,' said Deva.

'Senguntha, I feel tomorrow could be the moving day in the war. Rest well,' said Muruga and patted his friend's back. The three of them then retired to their respective quarters.

A new dawn, a new battle, and a new warrior awaited Muruga and the Ganas. Agnimugan blew the conch to signal the start of the day's battle. He wasn't just an accomplished warrior but also an expert flame thrower. He unleashed burning arrows in all directions and started blowing fire too. It was like a raging inferno spewing lava on hapless people. The Ganas were consumed by flames like shrubs in a forest fire. The onslaught by Agnimugan turned the battlefield into a volcanic rubble with charred remains of chariots, animals, and people. The warriors from both sides were losing their morale. The death toll was immense over the last few days.

Senguntha rode to the front in his chariot and confronted Agnimugan.

'You swine! I have been waiting for you. I will burn you to ashes and take it to my father,' roared Agnimugan.

'Your brother ran away yesterday. It's your turn today. Stop the empty talk and fight,' retorted Senguntha.

The battle began, with both warriors unleashing a flurry of arrows at each other and nullifying one another's attack. Agnimugan escalated the fight by shooting flaming arrows at Senguntha's horses and chariot. The charioteer fled on seeing the flaming arrows being targeted on him and the chariot. The horses bolted and soon the chariot was consumed by flames. Senguntha made a giant leap and landed on the ground. At this rate Agnimugan would destroy the entire Gana and Sura Army. Senguntha needed help and he sent word to Muruga and a set of ten elephants carrying huge drums of water came from Hemakootam to support Senguntha. They would extinguish the flame emanating from the arrows sent by Agnimugan by sprinkling water on them, while Senguntha tackled the arrows.

Agnimugan decided to invoke his family deity *Bhadra Kali.* She represented the most ferocious form of Goddess Shakthi. Sooran and Maya had taught him the art of sorcery from a very young age, which involved making sacrifices to Kali. Two Kali's appeared beside him, one to his right and one to his left, their tongue jutting out and dripping with blood. Flames crowned Agnimugan's head, and with Kali's besides, the sight alone could have killed many. Senguntha couldn't discern whether it was real or an illusion. He grasped the Rudraksha gifted by Swayambhu and began reciting the Maha Mritunjaya Mantra

|| *OM TRYAMBAKAM YAJAMAHE SUGANDHIM PUSHTI VARDHANAM*

URVARUKAMIVA BANDHANAN MRYTYOR MUKSHEEYA MAMRITAT ||

Within minutes, the image of the Kali's vanished, leaving Agnimugan stunned. He had always believed that the power of sorcery surpassed any other form of worship. He now realized that the power of true devotion could also serve as a protective shield. Determined to finish the battle, he decided to confront Senguntha once more. The battle continued with both warriors nullifying each other with their respective arrows. Agnimugan wasn't a seasoned warrior, hence not battle-hardened. The effort that he had put in crushing Muruga's army was taking its toll. Senguntha was also weak, having just recovered from a life-threating coma. Senguntha summoned all his strength, and prayed to his family deity, Veerabhadra and let go of an arrow. It found its mark. The arrow pierced Agnimugan's chest, splattering blood across his face. The weapons force threw him several feet away and he bled to his death.

There was great jubilation on the Gana's side, contrasted with the gloom on the Asura side. Sooran sank in his chair on hearing the news of Agnimugan's death. He wondered if this was the beginning of the end.

THE LAST THROW OF THE DICE

On hearing the news of his brother's death, Banukoban hurried to Sooran's private quarters to console his father. Sooran sat in a chair, hands on his head, lamenting the sacrifices he had made for his blind pride.

By now, Banukoban had grasped the impending doom that was about to befall the Asura clan. He was a mighty warrior, but not foolish enough to ignore the writing on the wall. He wanted to persuade his stubborn father to yield to the enemy's demands to ensure the clan's survival.

'*Appa*, I understand the pain you are going through over losing your sons. I have lost my brothers too,' said Banukoban in a softened voice.

Sooran looked up and saw his eldest son standing in front of him. He had not noticed Banukoban entering the chamber.

'Banukoba, I shouldn't have involved your brothers in the war. It was my battle, and I should have fought alone,' said Sooran, his eyes filled with tears.

'It's not your fault. It is the duty of princes to protect their king and kingdom; they are true martyrs,' said Banukoban.

'Even if I win this war, I will die of guilt for allowing my young children to sacrifice their lives for me,' said Sooran, overwhelmed with emotion.

'*Appa*, may I say something to you?' asked Banukoban.

'Speak freely, my son. You are not just my eldest, you are the crown prince of our clan,' Sooran said, composing himself.

'I believe we should be practical in our approach; the enemy is clearly more powerful than us. It's only a matter of time before we succumb. Let us accept their terms,' said Banukoban.

'Banukoba,' screamed Sooran, 'Are you out of your mind?' You are an Asura, not an ascetic. Asuras live and die with pride,' retorted an angry Sooran.

'Actions in the present affect the future. Besides being an Asura, I am also a future king, and I must consider our people's future as well,' replied Banukoban.

'Don't lecture me! I built this kingdom, and they are enjoying the fruits of my labour,' retorted Sooran.

'But *Appa...*' pleaded Banukoban.

'I would rather die than live with the humiliation, of surrendering to a young boy, an upstart, and becoming a laughingstock in front of the bloody Suras,' Sooran said angrily.

'Muruga is not a young boy. Please understand our current situation. I am the only prince alive. Doesn't that show you the reality?' pleaded Banukoban.

'I understand your point of view very well, now. Go back to your palace, save yourself and your family. I will fight my own battles. I don't need your help,' said Sooran sarcastically.

'I am not a coward. I was only trying to give you my perspective of the war. I am here to obey your command. I will go to war as you wish,' said Banukoban, puffing out his chest.

'Now you are talking like Sooran's son. Go and finish them, and bring glory to our clan,' said Sooran, hugging Banukoban.

Banukoban touched his father's feet and left Sooran's private quarters.

The next day, Banukoban arrived at the northern frontier, ready for one final assault that would end the battle one way or the other. He sounded his bugle to signal the start of the day's battle, the Ganas who recognized the sound, knew their sworn enemy had returned. Before they could lose their morale, their supreme commander Senguntha rode past them like a gust of wind and stopped his chariot in front of Banukoban. Seeing Senguntha, Banukoban's blood boiled. He couldn't stand the sight of his brother's murderer still alive, even after he had put him into a coma.

'Welcome back from the dead, my friend! You somehow survived the coma, but this time I will ensure that your flesh is fed to the sharks,' Banukoban blurted out in rage.

Just as he finished speaking, he launched a flurry of arrows towards Senguntha, who swatted them away with his own set of arrows. They had already used the *Shivastram* against each other and it couldn't be used again according to the principles of war. This would be a battle of attrition until one of them perished– a true test of skills, endurance, courage and risk-taking.

Banukoban knew that simply firing arrows at Senguntha wouldn't be effective. He decided to combine sorcery with warfare. He would fire a set of arrows at Senguntha and disappear, making it hard for Senguntha's arrows to find their mark. He would appear in front of Senguntha, sometimes to his right, sometimes to the left of Senguntha. Being a master warrior himself, Senguntha swiftly moved to his right and left, defending against the arrows. Banukoba then decided to change tactics. He would disappear, reappear and attack with different weapons each time. This unexpected strategy began to turn the battle in his favour, as Senguntha was wounded by the various weapons. Senguntha knew he needed help, or he would lose this battle soon, and possibly be killed. He closed his eyes for a moment, praying to Muruga.

Sensing that Senguntha was weakening, Banukoban confidently appeared before him and fired another set of arrows that pierced Senguntha's armour, hitting his chest. Senguntha had to keep fighting and hope that help would arrive, and it did! A spear, coming out of the blue, crashed into Banukoban's shoulder, momentarily immobilizing him. Senguntha turned around to see Muruga standing next to him on his chariot.

Seizing the opportunity, Senguntha leaped into the air and severed Banukoban's left hand with one swift move. Banukoban plucked the spear embedded on his left shoulder and hurled it with his right hand onto Senguntha, who swiftly parried it and severed Banukoban's right hand too. The crown prince of Mahendrapuri stood there with no hands, bleeding profusely. He knew the end was near and glanced at Muruga as if to say it wasn't fair. With one stroke of his sword, Senguntha beheaded Banukoban as the headless body fell at his feet.

The Gana warriors erupted in instant celebration. This was a body blow to Sooran and his Asura warriors. One of their most powerful warlords lay dead, which would not only weaken the morale of the soldiers but also emotionally devastate Sooran. The crown prince, his eldest and most powerful son, was dead.

The news spread like wildfire and soon reached the king of Mahendrapuri. Sooran fell from his chair upon hearing it, letting out a huge cry of lament. In every family, the eldest son had the right to perform the last rites of his parents. Now, he would have to perform the last rites for his eldest son. It was a very poignant moment for any parent. Sooran was now at cross roads. Was he leading the Asura clan to total destruction? Not only was he losing the war, but he was also losing his entire family. He was torn between Kshatriya pride and love for the family, but ultimately, pride for a Kshatriya was always larger than life, and it prevailed.

Sooran sent word through his guards to awaken Simhan. Simhan was no ordinary being, he was literally a giant. As a newborn, he was larger than a ten-year-old child. He spent most of his time eating and sleeping. It wasn't easy to wake Simhan up. Ear-splitting sounds were needed to rouse him. The entourage did everything to wake him. After hours of cacophony, they finally succeeded. He was about to crush the musicians when one of them handed him a palm-leaf manuscript containing Sooran's orders to come immediately. Simhan stood up and rushed to Sooran's palace.

Simhan ran into Sooran's private quarters, yelling *'Anna... Anna...'*

'I heard the news about Banukoban. You should have called me earlier. I warned you about Muruga; he is no ordinary boy. He destroyed Tharakan and *Krauncha Malai*; that should tell you something,' said a perturbed Simhan.

'Are you saying, I should be scared?' retorted Sooran. 'I am only saying, be realistic,' said Simhan calmly.

'The only realism I know is that you have been sleeping while we are at war,' said Sooran sarcastically.

'Better late than never. I will confront Muruga and crush him. If I don't return, remember what I've told you and make a wise decision,' said Simhan.

'Simha...'

'Do you not trust your own ability?' roared Sooran.

'It's not about trusting my ability; it's about understanding the power of the enemy. There are invisible forces beyond those on the battlefield driving this war. You just need to see it!' Simhan said philosophically.

'Are you not ashamed to talk like this, as an Asura? Where is your pride?' retorted Sooran.

'My Asura pride is in place, that's precisely why I told you, I will lead the front line. Bless me, brother,' said Simhan, bowing down to Sooran.

'Victory will be yours, my brother,' replied Sooran, raising his hand in a gesture of blessing.

Simhan let out a thunderous roar that shook the entire palace, and proceeded toward the northern front. He sounded his bugle, which was so loud that it caused a mild tremor on the earth. The Gana warriors were stunned to see a giant standing in front of them. One of the soldiers ran to Muruga and informed him that a giant had now stepped into the field.

Senguntha, who stood near Muruga felt it must be Simhan, who had come to the battlefield. He sought Muruga's blessings to take on Simhan.

'If that's your wish, I won't stop you. Go ahead,' said Muruga, wishing his friend good luck.

Senguntha brought his chariot in front of Simhan. He was astounded by the size of the man in front of him. He had never seen anyone of that size before. Being a

warrior, he didn't flinch. He took out his conch and blew it to signal the start of the battle.

Simhan started throwing giant boulders and huge trees at the Gana army. They were being crushed. Simhan trampled a few that were close to him and crushed some of them with his bare hands. This was warfare that the Ganas never anticipated, and they were retreating in hordes as more boulders fell on them.

Senguntha fired a set of arrows at Simhan, who caught them like toys and broke them into pieces. Simhan himself fired a set of arrows that killed warriors en masse, including Visali, Senguntha's charioteer. Senguntha fired the *Veerabhadra Asthiram* on Simhan; it caused only a minor wound on his chest. Simhan then threw a huge boulder at Senguntha that broke his chariot into pieces. Senguntha had anticipated the attack and just in the nick of time, jumped onto a tree nearby. Senguntha realized his folly and arrogance. This was Muruga's way of teaching him a lesson.

Seeing no one in front of him, Simhan thumped his chest and let out a victory roar.

'Cowards! Where is that boy? Is he hiding in the barracks? I will go and kill him there,' said a fuming Simhan.

Simhan began moving forward with his giant frame, towards the barracks. Suddenly, he saw a white elephant approaching him with agility and grace at the same time. He stood still for a moment as the elephant stopped in front of him.

'Are you looking for me?' said the warrior seated on the elephant. It was Muruga riding on Airavatha.

'Ha Ha!! Are you the baby-faced warrior?' asked Simhan in disdain.

'Correct yourself! I am neither a child nor a warrior; I am the commander-in-chief of this army,' said Muruga nonchalantly.

'*Kuzhanthaai,*' said Simhan very sweetly, addressing Muruga as a child.

'We have a long-standing enmity with the Suras, and as per the Kshatriya Dharma, we have to fight for our clan. You are not a Sura; you are Swayambhu's son. Why are you fighting for the Suras? Go back to where you belong.'

'Well, you are following your Dharma, I am following mine. Didn't Krishna take sides when the Kurus were fighting amongst each other? They were part of the same family, so are the Suras and you,' said Muruga with conviction.

'So, you believe you are God? Krishna was an Avatar; you are just a human,' chided Simhan.

'Perhaps, you haven't heard of the phrase, *Devo Manushya Rupena, God revealed through human form*,' said Muruga calmly.

'You seem to be more a philosopher than a warrior,' said Simhan with a chuckle.

'War requires both acumen and *asthras*, they are the duality that define warfare,' said Muruga.

'Fair enough, Wise Warrior! We shall see; prepare to fight,' said Simhan.

It looked like a fight between a giant and a pigmy, however, there is a saying that even an ant can traumatize an elephant if it enters its ear.

Both warriors took their positions. Simhan was the first to strike. He threw a huge boulder at Muruga, who smashed it to pieces with his arrows. Now it was Muruga's turn. He pulled out twelve arrows from his quiver and shot them at once. The twelve arrows took the shape of a bow as they were fired and slammed into Simhan's right, neck down to his legs. A shocked Simhan plucked out the arrows one by one and broke them to pieces, even though he was bleeding. While he was removing the arrows on his right side, another set of arrows hit him on the left side top down. He repeated the act of removing the arrows on the left side as well, with some flesh dangling from them.

A fuming Simhan decided to opt for sorcery. He took the form of a ten-headed man. It was like a giant Ravana standing in front of Muruga. Muruga knew it was an illusion but decided to continue his fight. He took aim for one of the heads with his arrows and severed it; another one came in its place on the other side.

This pattern went on for a while. Muruga would rip apart one head, and another would come again. The Gana warriors were getting restless; if Muruga proved ineffective against Simhan, this could mean the end of the war.

Muruga remembered every system had a weak link, and every human had a weak body part. Since Simhan used Sorcery to showcase multiple heads, Muruga knew instinctively that the head was not his most vulnerable area. Muruga had an intuition. He took out his Shakthi *Vel* and aimed at Simhan's navel; it pierced the navel and tore his stomach. Now Simhan was truly in pain. The multiple heads disappeared, and Simhan was trying to remove the *Vel* that had pierced his stomach. It had gone so deep inside that if he attempted to remove it, it would probably mutilate him even more. Simhan picked up a massive sword and swiped at Muruga, who was too quick for him, the sword missed its mark. Muruga picked up another set of arrows and shot an arrow at Simhan's right eye blinding him. Blood came pouring out of the eye.

Bleeding from the stomach, and with only one eye, Simhan was now dizzy and unbalanced. He blindly swiped at Muruga with no effect. Muruga slid down the trunk of Airavatha and ran towards Simhan with swords in either hand. He slid between Simhan's legs, and with one swivel, stuck both knees from behind; they buckled, bringing the giant down to his knees.

Seizing the moment, Muruga jumped on to Simhan's back and sank his sword through the neck. The jugular vein snapped; Simhan coughed huge volumes of blood and fell face down, as Muruga stood on his back. It was a gory death for the mighty giant. Simhan's lifeless body lay on the battlefield, a testament to the fierce battle that had just taken place.

Muruga jumped down from the giant's back, bent down on one knee, went close to Simhan, and whispered in his ear, 'Lord Rudra bless your soul.'

THE FINAL ASSAULT

Sooran was up earlier than usual; he had mourned his beloved brother the previous night. Now, it was time to put an end to the war.

After his morning ablutions, he went to the prayer hall, applied *vibuthi* on his forehead and arms, and was ready to say his prayer. He showered flowers on the lingam, the main deity in the prayer hall. He bowed to Lord Shiva and sought his blessings. Besides the large lingam in the next sanctum sanctorum was a statue of Maya, his beloved mother. He showered flowers on his mother's statue, prostrated before it, and sought her blessings. Lastly, he prayed to Goddess Kali. There was a lamb tied to a tether in front of the Kali statue. Sooran raised his hands and a local priest beheaded the lamb as a sacrifice to Goddess Kali. Sooran hoped he would be able to provide a human sacrifice to Goddess Kali tomorrow, after today's battle.

Sooran had already sent word to all the kingdoms under his aegis to ensure that their respective armies assemble outside the Mahendrapuri fort. As Sooran stepped out of his palace, Padmakomalai applied red vermilion to his forehead and wished him success. He tapped her shoulder and hurriedly left, walking across the giant lawns. He climbed into his chariot and instructed his charioteer to head to the northern frontier. As the gates of the fort opened, he saw the assembled armies of all the kingdoms awaiting his instruction. He made his way through the sea of warriors and reached the front. Sooran and his massive army marched to the war zone.

Sooran and his golden chariot dazzled under the sun. The Gana army stood there, awestruck by the chariot and Sooran's presence. However, they knew in their hearts that today would be the day, the war ended. They believed in their hero, Muruga - destiny's child according to them, born to defeat Sooran in battle. Sooran had his chariot taken to the front of the warzone. Once there, he sounded his bugle to signal the beginning of the war. The Asura army also sounded different instruments to create a thunderous environment, lifting their morale.

On the opposite side was the dashing young man, ready to deliver justice to the Suras against Sooran, the most powerful man among all the clans besides his father Swayambhu. Muruga didn't need a golden chariot to shine in the sunlight. His face epitomized radiance. He was a mix of beauty, brawn, and brilliance that southern India had never seen before. Even Sooran gazed at him in awe. Muruga took out his conch and blew it, signalling that he and his army were also ready for battle.

Sooran initiated the attack on Muruga with a flurry of arrows. Muruga countered them with his own arrows. Sooran then threw a small-tipped spear at Muruga, who brought it down with his arrows. Sooran jumped out of his chariot and ran towards Muruga. Muruga calmly jumped off his chariot and ran towards the surging Sooran, who struck him with his sword. Muruga had already drawn his sword from his scabbard in anticipation and blocked the attack. A severe sword fight ensued between the two warriors. Sooran had more physical strength, but Muruga was agile and fleet-footed. After a while, Sooran decided it was time for sorcery.

Sooran vanished into thin air. After a few minutes there was blue smoke, and from within it, Sooran re-appeared sitting on a giant *chakravakam, ruddy goose.* Muruga was not fooled by the illusion and decided to play the game Sooran had started. Muruga disappeared and reappeared on a giant peacock. Sooran was taken a back. '*This boy is not only highly skilled in warfare but in sorcery too,*' he muttered to himself. The two warriors slid down their respective *vahanams or* vehicles. The peacock flew up, landing its claws on the ruddy goose slitting its neck. Within seconds there was a loud bang, and both birds disappeared.

Sooran now decided to up the ante; he brought forward the weapon that no one else had in the entire southern peninsula, including the kingdoms of Kadaram and Javam. It was the *Pasupathasthram,* the most powerful weapon unearthed from the kingdom of Lanka, said to have been possessed by Indrajit, the son of Ravan. A powerful missile that could cause total destruction. No one had a counter to this weapon.

Muruga drew an arrow from his quiver, the one he had discovered while praying to Lord Shiva at Sathya Giri near the Manni river. The arrow shone brightly blinding everyone nearby. Sooran's jaw dropped in astonishment. He felt it was an illusion as Muruga had already demonstrated his sorcery. Sooran asked his charioteer to turn around and leave the battlefield. Muruga pursued Sooran in his chariot until they reached the edge of the ocean. Senguntha followed Muruga in his chariot. He would never leave Muruga alone.

'Muruga, if you truly possess the *Pasupathasthram*, it is providence. Though I don't believe it, I wanted to check it out with minimal destruction, so I rode away from the army,' said Sooran.

'Soora, you are kind hearted after all; I pursued you, knowing very well, you would reach the ocean,' Muruga said nonchalantly.

Both the warriors released their arrows from their bow strings towards the ocean. There was a huge cloud burst with flames and smoke as the arrows collided and eventually fell into the sea. Total destruction was averted.

'Muruga, it seems the Gods are with you. However, I am Sooran, and even if I have to fight the gods to win, I will,' Sooran said, thumping his chest.

'The Gods are with all of us; we just need the vision to see it,' said Muruga.

'Stop patronizing me! Let's see how good you are,' said Sooran with disdain.

Sooran transformed himself into a red rooster using the ancient yogic technique of '*para kaya pravesam*' – the power of entering another body. Muruga transformed into a white rooster and the fight ensued. The two roosters went after each other. They would take two steps back and charge at each other. This continued for several rounds till Sooran returned to his original form with bruises all over his body. Sooran now turned himself into a tiger and jumped onto Muruga. Muruga invoked Lord Ganesha and transformed into a huge tusker. In the fight that ensued between the tusker and tiger, The tusker emerged victorious. It lifted the tiger and threw it in the air with its trunk. The tiger crashed to the earth some distance away. Sooran returned to his original form badly wounded and bruised. He was not going to give in.

Sooran decided to fight his last battle in his own form without shape-shifting. He lifted his sword and ran towards Muruga, who had also returned to his original form. Muruga decided to use the Shakthi *Vel*. Sooran took a swipe at Muruga's head, who swiftly sat down parrying the attack. Sparks flew as the weapons clashed. Sooran tried to Stab Muruga in his abdomen, but Muruga quickly brought his *Vel* in defense. Muruga rotated his *Vel* at a furious pace and advancing forward. Sooran couldn't keep up the defense with his shield. Muruga swerved to his right and shifted the *Vel* to his left, and disarmed Sooran. Sooran realized Muruga was ambidextrous, but it was too late.

Sooran had no protective shield now. Muruga continued to rotate his *Vel* and began circling Sooran as well. The speed and movement were so rapid that it looked like Sooran was engulfed in a dust storm created by a typhoon. Trying to keep pace with the rotation and revolution of Muruga, Sooran lost his balance and fell down. He stuttered as he got up. Sooran would charge forward in desperation and Muruga would simply side step, and Sooran would fall on the other side. This happened a few times.

Sooran was completely exhausted but wouldn't give up. He was fighting purely with his adrenaline and killer instinct. He let out a huge roar as he hurled his sword at Muruga. Muruga leapt in the air to avoid the Sword and flung the *Vel* at Sooran, which crashed into his chest and pierced through the other side. Blood gushed out of his chest as Sooran lay on the ground, thrown a fair distance by the power of the Shakthi *Vel*. He knew the end was near.

Muruga walked towards the dying soul as Sooran looked at him with reverence.

'*Ayyane*, it is my good fortune to be killed by you,' said Sooran with tears in his eyes.

'Soora, your soul will not die, it is your physical body that is dying,' said Muruga.

'I hope, I am born as a noble soul at least in my next birth. Will you grant me that wish?' asked Sooran with folded hands.

'I am no one to grant your wish, your karma will decide your future, as my karma will decide mine,' said Muruga.

'In the ages to come, you will probably be one of our Gods. I know the Suras already worship you,' said Sooran.

'*Naan Kadavul Neeyum Kadavul*,' *I am God, and so are you.*

Muruga continued, 'The divine drives us from within and the divine provides for us from the outside.'

'I have only one final request my Lord. Help me and the future generations understand the wisdom of life,' asked Sooran with folded hands.

'I will fulfil your last wish, great warrior,' said Muruga.

Muruga began to address Sooran. On his death bed Sooran was seeking enlightenment.

'During our battle, there were two important moments, and I would use them to explain the wisdom of life. I would also carry them as my symbols henceforth, for the benefit of the future generations as per your last wish.'

'In the first battle we became roosters and fought against each other. The rooster keeps reminding us every morning to rise from darkness and move towards light. This signifies that one should always move from ignorance to the knowledge of the divine.'

My favourite bird is the peacock. It has its days of splendour and days that it is bereft of its beautiful feathers. This represents the cycle of life. We will have good days and bad days, but the good days will return, just like the peacock regrows its feathers. Life and Death are also like Good and bad days; one follows the other.'

Sooran felt blessed hearing these words, as he drew one last breath and succumbed to *Yama's* call, the god of death had finally come to take him.

Muruga lifted Sooran's body and put it on his chariot and rode back to the war zone. As Muruga's chariot entered the war zone, the stunned Asura warriors immediately dropped their weapons in surrender. Their king had been vanquished, and the war was over.

As the supreme commander of the Gana Army rode past them, they ran behind it to catch the last glimpse of their king. The mighty Sooran was no more, unthinkable yet the reality in front of them. The Gana warriors were shouting in jubilation at their victory. They had succeeded in the mission led by the mighty Muruga.

Muruga, raised his hands and the Ganas stopped their jubilation. Muruga asked Senguntha to come with a decorated chariot. Soon Senguntha arrived at the war zone as instructed by Muruga. He helped Muruga lay the motionless body of Sooran on the decorated chariot.

Muruga addressed both the armies together.

'Dear Comrades, let us all follow the path of Dharma and use our strength and power for the welfare of everyone, the Asura army is free to return home.'

The Suras, Ganas, and Asuras were all stunned. Unlike Sooran or Deva, who would have boasted if they had won this battle, Muruga remained humble. He pardoned the opponents and asked everyone to follow the lessons learnt from this war. He was one of his kind, probably the world would never see again. They felt blessed to have been part of this war and to be in the presence of Muruga.

The Asura army left silently behind the chariot carrying their once mighty king. As the chariot rolled into Mahendrapuri towards Sooran's palace, Padmakomalai, who had heard the news, ran out from the palace towards her dead husband. She stood there for a moment, looking at her lifeless husband, totally blank.

The chariot was parked at the centre of the city. The news of Sooran's death also reached Hiranyan, but out of fear of retribution from his own people, he decided not to return. Padmakomalai decided to break tradition and perform her husband's final rites herself. She would then walk into the pyre.

The last rites were completed and Padmakomalai looked around at the people paying their last respects. She bowed to them with folded hands and walked onto the burning pyre. It was the end of the Asura clan. Over centuries, civilizations were built and destroyed, kings and kingdoms rose and fell, but this was the greatest war the southern peninsula had seen, where an entire family had been eliminated.

Back at Hemakootam, Muruga was resting in his palace, sitting in *padmasan, lotus posture* in meditation. He prayed for the departed souls on both sides. After a while, he sent for Senguntha.

'Lord, you called me?' asked Senguntha.

'Yes, my dear friend. Go to Mahendrapuri tomorrow and release Jayanthan and the rest of the Suras held captive,' said Muruga.

'As you command, my lord,' replied Senguntha.

'We will also leave for Velliangiri immediately after your return. I am eager to meet my parents and then we shall go to Skandha Kottai,' said Muruga.

'I will send a pigeon courier to Lord Rishabha informing him about our return,' replied Senguntha.

The next day, Senguntha left with a hand full of soldiers to Mahendrapuri. He reminisced his earlier entry into Mahendrapuri.

There was no one to stop him or fight him this time. The people were closeted in their homes not knowing what would happen to them. Senguntha reached the prison, the guards escorted him to the cells where the Suras were imprisoned. Jayanthan was delighted to see Senguntha; he knew that Sooran had been defeated and Senguntha had come to free them all.

'Great warrior, you have kept your word. We are all indebted to you and Lord Muruga,' said Jayanthan.

'We were given a mission and we accomplished it under the leadership of Lord Muruga,' said Senguntha.

Jayanthan and the rest of the Suras were escorted out of the prison. The Suras were put in several caravans while Jayanthan boarded Senguntha's chariot, and the entourage left for Hemakootam.

Deva waited with bated breath to see his son. As soon as he saw the chariot entering Hemakootam, Deva rushed towards it. Jayanthan jumped off the chariot and ran towards his father. Both embraced each other, tears flowing from their eyes. The joy knew no bounds. All the Suras got down from the caravans and knelt before their king. Deva asked Jayanthan to go meet Muruga.

Muruga was in his abode as Jayanthan ran and prostrated in front of him.

'You are a future King, don't fall at my feet, Rule well. May Lord Shiva be with you,' said Muruga and lifted him up.

Muruga had come, seen, and conquered everyone's mind, heart, and Sooran. The warrior had accomplished his mission. It was now time to head home. He had to seek his parents' blessings on returning victorious. There was also a surprise that awaited him.

THE HOLY UNION

Senguntha led the entourage back along the original route, stopping at Senthilpuri, a place Muruga considered his second home. Muruga wanted to rest for the night at Senthilpuri, captivated by the location's tranquillity. He went to his abode, climbed to the terrace, and lay on a silk mat. Gazing at the stars above, he felt one with the universe.

Meanwhile, the army created a huge bonfire on the beach to celebrate their victory with balladry. Among them was Gandharva, one of the released Suras held captive by Banukoban. He was a well-trained musician and poet who began to write and sing the soldiers' stories as they reminisced their journey. The enthusiasm of released Suras energized the soldiers, and the festivities continued through the night by the sand and sea.

As the night celebrations waned and dawn approached, Deva gathered everyone to make an important announcement.

'Thanks to Muruga, we have our lives back. He fought an iconic war that the world will remember. Gandharva has poetically chronicled the journey of Muruga. We, the Suras, will celebrate this occasion every year, starting on the sixth day of *Karthigai* month, with six days of festivities culminating in a dance drama depicting Sooran's defeat by Muruga.'

It shall be called '*Soora Samaharam*.'

The entire army erupted with cries of '*Aro Hara Aro Hara*!'

Deva had sent a pigeon courier to Sachi the previous night informing her about Sooran's death at Muruga's hands and the release of their son Janyanthan. He urged her to visit Velliangiri and inform Swayambhu and Shakthi about the good news. He also detailed the plans for Muruga's surprise gift.

The entourage began their journey back to their motherland. Despite the long journey, no one felt fatigued. There was camaraderie, enthusiasm, and banter all around– telltale signs of a victorious team.

Meanwhile, Velliangiri was abuzz after Sachi conveyed the news to Muruga's proud parents. She also briefed them on the planned surprise for Muruga. Overjoyed by the plan, they decided to be part of it.

After a long journey, Muruga and his army arrived at Thiruparankunram, the place of Umai Andavar. The hermits, who had been awaiting them, since their return from Senthilpuri, greeted them with Vedic hymns and praises of Lord Shiva. Muruga dismounted from his chariot and bent down to touch their feet. They blessed him *'Vaazhga Valathudan' meaning live prosperously.*

Since Muruga had achieved a victory against the mighty Sooran, they suggested he offer prayers to Lord Umai Andavar, as a thanksgiving to Lord Shiva. They also noted that this was the place of the Pandavas, the clan that emerged victorious against the Kauravas and Adharma. Muruga, respecting the wishes of the hermits, bowed with reverence and agreed to perform a *homam* to Lord Umai Andavar the next day.

The next day Muruga prepared himself, and reached the sanctum sanctorum of Umai Andavar. To his surprise, he saw Swayambhu, Shakthi, and Sachi there. Muruga was thrilled to bits and prostrated before his parents. Swayambhu lifted him up and hugged him, while Shakthi, eyes filled with tears of joy, embraced her victorious son. Sachi blessed him too.

Deva walked in with his daughter Amrutha behind him. She was petite, fair-skinned, and draped in a glittering white saree and a golden blouse. A diamond *vangi* adorned her biceps, a diamond necklace graced her neck, and dazzling diamond rings embellished her ears. She looked like one of the *apsaras* from heaven. Her head down, too shy to meet Muruga's gaze.

'Dear Muruga, I hereby offer my daughter's hand to you in marriage. Please accept her,' said Deva.

'Muruga looked deeply into Deva's eyes, his voice filled with sincerity: I accept your daughter's hand in marriage as I promised in Velliangiri, now that my mission is accomplished,' said Muruga.

Amrutha stood there, half blushing and half shy, her cheeks turning pink. She looked up at her beloved for the first time, and Muruga met her gaze. It was truly a match made in heaven.

A simple ceremony was arranged at the temple of Umai Andavar to formalize the marriage of Amrutha, and Muruga. Prajapathi arrived in time to lead the marriage rituals, also in attendance were Krithika, Chandra, Sundara, and Kamala. The sacred fire was lit in a *homa kundam* as Muruga recited the marriage mantras. Following tradition, Sundara gave a garland to Muruga, who placed it around Amrutha's neck. She received her garland from Prajwal, placing it around Muruga's neck. The temple bells tolled as Rishabha played the Mridangam, Vani played the Vana, and the Ganas blew their conches. Amidst the musical symphony and with the blessings of all the friends and relatives, Muruga tied the *thirumangalyam, the sacred thread* around Amrutha sanctifying their union in the presence of Agni, the God of Fire. The holy union was complete after they performed the *sapthapathi, seven rounds* around the sacred fire.

After the marriage rituals ended, the entourage of the Ganas and Suras prepared to leave for Velliangiri. As per Muruga's wishes, he and his wife were allowed to travel back to Senthilpuri. Pawan offered to be their charioteer, but Muruga told him he had done enough service during the war and should be with his family. Muruga chose to be the charioteer, with his wife behind him, signifying his new role as a family man.

Muruga and Amrutha took the blessings of all the elders and drove towards the scenic Senthil Puri.

Once they reached Senthilpuri, Amrutha fell in love with the place, just as Muruga had. Muruga and his bride decided to stroll on the beach. Senthilpuri had already captivated Muruga, and walking hand in hand with his wife made the place look even more heavenly. The shy and reticent Amrutha walked silently beside Muruga, her toes tracing delicate patterns in the sand. Muruga, meanwhile, absorbed the serene beauty of the surroundings and the comforting presence of his new bride.

Amrutha wanted to start a conversation, to understand her husband's likes and dislikes but was hesitant. She had grown up very protected and knew little about worldly affairs. Finally, she mustered the courage to speak.

'*Natha*, may I ask you something?' said Amrutha in her tender voice.

'*Priye*, you don't need permission to talk to me. We are bound together in holy matrimony, blessed by the gods,' said Muruga.

'I hear you are the bravest warrior and the brightest mind. I don't know if I am even worthy of having you as my husband,' said Amrutha in awe.

'I am the privileged one, not you, as I have the greatest beauty across all of our clans as my wedded wife,' said Muruga with a twinkle in his eyes.

Amrutha's face turned pink, like a lotus. She covered her face and tried to run away, but Muruga grabbed her hand and pulled her towards him, resulting in an embrace. Against the backdrop of the setting sun, the silhouette of two lovers in embrace stood.

In the bliss of the moonlight, they remain embraced, losing track of time. Muruga then released Amrutha and held her chin, looking deep into her eyes. She hung her head shyly, but Muruga lifted her chin and kissed her lips. Hand in hand, they moved towards Muruga's Sea abode. The gentle sound of waves crashing on the shore accompanied their steps, and the wooden door closed behind them with a soft creak, sealing their moment of privacy.

Far away in Swarga, Vishwakarman, who had left immediately after the wedding, was overseeing the preparations for a grand reception that would include all the kings under the Asuras, the Sura aristocracy, and the Gana aristocracy. Deva, having attended Swayambhu and Shakthi's re-union, wanted the grand reception for his daughter and son-in-law to be at least ten times grander, as he was the wealthiest man in town.

Meanwhile at Velliangiri, Prajapathi discussed with Swayambhu on the way forward for the Asura clan, as Swayambhu was the Supreme Lord of all the clans.

Swayambhu suggested that Deva should be coronated just like Sooran to provide good governance to both the Suras and Asuras, after all they were cousins. Prajapathi suggested that the coronation could follow the grand reception being planned in Swarga for the newly wedded couple.

Two days later, Muruga and Amrutha arrived at Swarga. Amrutha looked more jaded than Muruga after the nights spent at Senthilpuri and the long journey back home. Sachi and Kamala came to perform the traditional *aarthi,* to ward off evil eyes from the couple. Muruga then went to rest in the guest room of the grand palace, as the grand reception was planned for the evening, and both needed to rest well.

An ensemble of events was planned for the evening. It opened with *mangala isai, holy music,* followed by a classical music recital of Vani on the Vana and Rishabha on the Mridangam. It was followed by a dance drama depicting the Soora Samaharam enacted by Swayambhu and Shakthi, who were deeply involved in presenting the valorous deeds of their son. This was followed by a dance performance by the bride herself, a trained dancer. Muruga enjoyed every gesture, the poise, and grace of the beautiful Amruthavalli, unable to take his eyes off her even for a moment.

Senguntha, who was sitting beside Muruga, was roasting his friend on becoming an incurable romantic.

Amrutha's dance performance was followed by the best court dancers of the Sura Clan: Ramba, Oorvasi, and Menaka, who depicted the greatness of the Suras and how they provided all the essential elements of life for all the other clans. The festivities continued with a grand feast prepared by Nala, featuring twenty varieties of savouries and twenty-five varieties of sweets. Guests were left licking their hands even after multiple servings. Somapanam flowed abundantly, causing some to faint from overconsumption. The revelry continued throughout the night.

Deva thanked all the guests as they retired to the quarters allocated to them, while some left for their respective homes. While seeing off the guests, a soldier informed Deva that Swayambhu had requested to see him in his quarters.

Deva immediately rushed to see him, as he was not only the Supreme Lord of all the clans but also his *sambandi, daughters' parent-in-law.* Deva was ready to do anything for Swayambhu now that his daughter was part of the Gana family.

'Lord, you wanted to see me?' asked Deva.

'The time has come for you to be coronated as the king of kings to rule and govern the Suras, Asuras, and the subservient clans. I have asked Prajapathi to find an auspicious date and time,' said Swayambhu.

'Your wish is my command,' said Deva, bending down to touch Swayambhu's feet and seek his blessings while thanking Muruga in silence.

DEVA'S CORONATION & THEREAFTER

Indraprastha, once glittering with gold and diamonds, had turned into a ghost town filled with dilapidated buildings and burnt-out houses, devoid of any inhabitants.

Vishwakarman was tasked with rebuilding the city to its past glory before Deva's coronation as *Chakravarthi*. This wasn't going to be an easy task. It was decided that hospitals and schools would be prioritized over the rest of the buildings. A grand community hall would be built, which would also serve as the *mandapam* for the coronation. Extra labourers, animals, and the best technology available were deployed to complete this monumental task.

Muruga decided to visit Indraprastha to motivate the workers and boost Vishwakarman's morale. He was accompanied by his newly wedded bride, Amrutha. Though she was saddened by the city's condition, she wished to see it restored to its former glory as soon as possible.

After several months of painstaking effort, Indraprastha was gradually regaining its former glory, with buildings springing up in every corner. People had already started moving back into their renovated homes or makeshift homes while setting up new ones. With the coronation date approaching, the city was abuzz with activity. The entire city was adorned with garlands and decorations, creating a festive atmosphere.

After a long time, the citizens had regained their city, lives and livelihood and the excitement was very palpable.

Muruga, Amrutha, Senguntha, Pawan, and Prajwal arrived three days before the coronation. They decorated the palace beautifully with white and purple cloth running across the length and breadth of the palace, complemented by green satin ribbons crisscrossing them. Amrutha along with some of her friends drew intricate *kolams* in front of the palace and decorated them with colourful flowers. The air was filled with the captivating scent of sandalwood and other herbal powders, making people feel as though they were in paradise.

The coronation day arrived. Prajapathi led the rituals to be performed to crown Deva as king of kings, with Swayambhu anointed to place the crown on Deva. Airavatha halted in front of the grand palace of Indraprastha. The mahout instructed the elephant to kneel, and Deva dismounted amidst the deafening sound of bugles, conches, and cymbals being rendered.

Deva walked on the pathway of flowers from the entrance to the throne inside the King's court. As he walked with Sachi, Muruga, Amrutha, Pawan, Prajwal, and Varun, the palace maids showered rose petals on them welcoming their king and queen. Thousands watched as the grand event unfolded. The heyday of the Suras had well and truly arrived. At the entrance of the king's court, Kamala and Shakthi were ready to perform the *aarthi* as part of the traditional welcome before Deva and Sachi entered the court.

Chants of '*Devaraja Vaazhga, Surendran Vaazhga!*' filled the air as Deva and Saachi entered the courtroom. It was filled to capacity with his ministers and advisors. Jayanthan sat on a small throne meant for the prince, beside the mammoth throne that awaited its king. The Brahmanas had arrived early and were reciting vedic hymns as Deva made his way to the throne. Swayambhu sat in a special throne next to the King. As per custom, Sachi went upstairs to sit in the designated places for the queens and princesses. They would watch the proceedings from there.

At the stroke of *muhurtham*, the most auspicious time for coronation, Prajapathi asked Swayambhu to step forward and place the *navarathna kireedam,* the crown studded with nine jewels on Deva's head. As the crown was being placed, everyone showered rose petals on the king of kings as a mark of respect, good wishes and blessings. Deva was now the *Chakravarthi*, a mighty one at that, as he had Muruga as his son-in-law and commander-in- chief.

Deva pledged to rule all the clans in a just manner upholding Dharmic values. Swayambhu would continue to be the guiding light for all the clans as the most revered figure. Every *Chakravarthi* had a sceptre known as *Sengol,* a symbol of the Supreme Leadership. Vishwakarman had crafted a unique sceptre for Deva.

It was shaped like a rod of lightning. Prajapathi had christened the sceptre as *Vajra*. He handed the sceptre to Deva who held it aloft in his right hand. Deafening sounds of '*Surapathi Vaazhga, Devarajan Vaazhga!*' filled the air.

Under Devarajan's rule, Indraprastha regained its eminence. Glittering palaces and gigantic households sprang up all over the city attracting visitors from across the land, including tourists and traders, with some making it their new home. Across the sea, Mahendrapuri also thrived due to its proximity to the seaport. Trade flourished, wealth grew, and the citizens were happy with peace and prosperity, free from war.

After a while, much like a mid-life crisis, something irked Deva, despite him executing his duties as a king to perfection. He began having nightmares about the humiliation suffered under Sooran and the ignominy of being called a puppet king by many in the sly, as Muruga helped him win the war.

Muruga had moved to Skandha Kottai with Amrutha but visited his in-laws once a month to pay his respects and ensure Amrutha's happiness. During one such visit, Muruga noticed his father-in-law's uneasiness and decided to talk to him.

'*Mama*,' said Muruga, using a commonly used term to refer to one's father-in-law.

'Something seems to be troubling you deeply. You can share it with me,' said Muruga.

'Muruga, you perceive things much earlier than anyone else; you are truly gifted,' said Deva.

'A mother can tell if her child is hungry or sleepy just by looking at the child. It's the bond. Similarly, you are my father-in-law and Amrutha's happiness lies in your happiness, so I look out for you too,' said Muruga.

'I am haunted by nightmares of my humiliation and my inability to defend my kingdom, needing someone else's help to stay on the throne. I don't deserve being a *Chakravarthi*,' said Deva his voice filled with pain.

'*Mama*, you are overthinking. Bheeshma was defeated in the Kurukshetra war; does that make him incapable? Arjuna wouldn't have won without Krishna's help. Does that mean he doesn't deserve the win?' Muruga said calmly and with conviction.

'I feel like leaving everything and going to the forest to meditate on Lord Shiva for eternal salvation,' said Deva.

'*Mama*, everyone has a defined set of duties according to their Varna. You are a Kshatriya. A Kshatriya's duty is to protect, provide justice, maintain law and order, and enable businesses. If you leave to meditate, you will be failing in your duties as a king,' said Muruga.

'I understand my duties very well, but unfortunately, don't have the drive to lead anymore,' said Deva, sulking.

'Maybe it's time for you to let someone else lead but still provide the necessary advice, till they are ready to be on their own,' said Muruga.

'Great suggestion, Muruga. Let me hand over the Kingdom to my son Jayanthan. You can be his advisor, as you are very knowledgeable, while I take the path of *vanaprastha*,' said Deva, somewhat relieved.

Vanaprastha literally means heading to the forest. It is a stage in life when a man has completed all the obligations to his family and is now free to let go of the bond.

'What will you accomplish by going into the forest?' asked Muruga.

'I will perform severe penance to Lord Shiva and seek salvation,' said Deva.

'Why do you believe that's the only way to salvation? Is renunciation the only way?' asked Muruga.

Deva didn't quite know how to answer; he was stumped as usual.

'Muruga, I am not good at answering your probing questions, and you know that. Please tell me what should I do?' asked Deva.

Muruga began explaining the principle of eternal salvation to Deva in detail.

Eternal salvation is not achieved merely by doing penance. Every *atma,* or soul, has a predetermined cycle, be it an insect, reptile, or human. Its actions in a particular birth determine its progression upwards or downwards in the evolutionary hierarchy. The human form is an evolution from the animal form, retaining all the animal traits with the addition of consciousness. The consciousness makes humans aware that they are part of an ongoing evolution and not the final state. When a human is truly conscious, it permeates his subconsciousness and helps in connecting with the super consciousness or the divine.

Our scriptures have defined four paths to reach the state of consciousness: they are Gnana Yoga, Bhakti Yoga, Karma Yoga, and Raja Yoga.

Gnana Yoga symbolizes the path of knowledge. It focuses on gaining knowledge about the Brahman through reading and understanding Vedic scriptures, reciting them constantly, and refraining from worldly pleasures. It involves questioning oneself: Who am I? Why am I here? What is my purpose in life? It is about reflecting, contemplating, sometimes just remaining in silence. The great sages followed this path. In the current world, it is most suited for the varna of Brahmans.

Bhakti Yoga symbolizes the path of devotion, focusing on building a connection with the divine through reciting prayers, worshipping nature, performing every task righteously with total devotion, and seeing divinity in every entity. Many individuals have exemplified Bhakti Yoga, none more than Hanuman. In the current world, this path is most suited for the varna of Vaishyas, whose responsibility is to provide for the poor & needy, and take care of the plants, *pashu,* and *pakshi*, pashu refers to all the animals and pakshi to all the birds.

Karma Yoga is the yoga of action. It involves performing actions without any attachment, focusing on *sevai,* or selfless service. In this path, one does not concern themselves with learning scriptures or performing rituals; it is pure service to everyone else. The scriptures state that the greatest service to the divine is to serve sages and bhaktas. Being born to serve others is considered a boon, as it pleases the divine the most. In our current scenario, this path is most suited for the varna of Shudras.

Raja Yoga, as the name suggests, is the path of the king, the royal path. In this path, just as a king maintains control over his kingdom, he exercises control over his mind. When the mind is disturbed, the divine self is obscured; when the mind is still, the *atma* shines from within. This is the essence of Raja Yoga. It requires having a balance in diet, sleep, lifestyle, and maintaining a state of equilibrium in victory and defeat. Raja Yoga allows a king to continue fulfilling his duties to his people while getting closer to the divine through a middle path between the material and spiritual. It is best suited for a Kshatriya.

Muruga concluded by saying,

'*Mama*, as I have mentioned above, your path to salvation is not in the forest through penance but being a good king following the path of Raja Yoga.'

Deva was speechless for a moment. His mind travelled back several centuries to the Kurukshetra war. He visualized himself as Arjuna and Muruga as Krishna sermonizing him in the midst of the war. The treatise of the Bhagwad Gita came in the middle of the physical war; he was receiving the treatise in the midst of his mental war.

'Muruga, you have opened my eyes. I shall continue until I am physically fit and follow the path of Raja Yoga,' said Deva, bowing to Muruga with hands folded in a *namaskaram*.

VELAN WEDS VALLI

It had been two years since Muruga's victorious battle against Sooran, and Deva's coronation as the king of kings. Muruga enjoyed a blissful married life while imparting his wisdom and skills to the Sura Army. Meanwhile, Senguntha had returned to Poigai to be with his mother after the war and all its celebrations, seeking peace in the comfort of his home and his mother's presence.

One evening, while strolling near the scenic mountains of Skandha kottai, Muruga encountered saint Rishiraja. Muruga immediately bowed down to him and sought his blessings. The saint blessed him with prosperity and long life.

'It is such a coincidence. I was on my way to meet you, and here you are,' said Rishiraja.

'It is such an honour to meet you. What can I do for you, revered one?' asked Muruga.

'You don't have to do anything for me; you should do it for yourself,' said Rishiraja.

'I am pretty happy with my life right now and content; there is nothing I yearn for,' said Muruga calmly.

'Some one yearns for you, and I think you should fulfil their wishes,' said Rishiraja with a smile.

Muruga was puzzled by Rishiraja's riddles, but he knew this was how the saint communicated. Though

Rishiraja's actions often caused confusion, they invariably led to good outcomes. Muruga chose to go with the flow.

'O great Rishi, if you could tell me the specifics, I could decide on the course of action,' said Muruga.

Rishiraja began to recount the tale of Nambi, a tribal king who lived in Vallimalai, a hillock near the town of Melpadi. The tribe's occupation was hunting, and they adhered to rigid practices. They remained a closed group, with marriages also happening within their tribe. They preferred to be isolated from the rest of the society. Nambi had long been childless and prayed daily to Lord Shiva for a child.

During one of his routine hunting trips, Nambi encountered a doe. As he was about to release his arrow, he looked into the doe's eyes and felt as though the doe was pleading for mercy. Realizing the doe might be a mother, Nambi had a change of heart and lowered his bow, allowing the doe to run away. A few days later, the doe appeared in front of his house. Bewildered, Nambi called for his wife Kodukki, who was inside doing her chores. She was thrilled to see a beautiful doe in her courtyard. The doe approached and tugged at Nambi's *angavastram, stole,* signalling him to follow her.

Nambi and Kodukki mounted their horses, and followed the doe deep into the forest, and soon found themselves on the other side of Vallimalai, arriving at a patch of tapioca called *Valli Kizhangu* by locals, which gave Vallimalai its name, the Tapioca Mountain. The doe slowed down and stopped near one of the pits where tapioca had been extracted. Nambi dismounted and went to inspect the pit. He sensed some movement and soon heard the cry of a baby. He looked closer and, lo and behold, there was a baby wrapped in a cloth inside the pit.

By then, Kodukki had dismounted her horse and reached the spot. Nambi lifted the baby from the pit and handed it to Kodukki. An overjoyed Kodukki held the baby in her hands, tears of joy streaming down her face. Overwhelmed with emotion, she hugged the baby against her bosom. Their prayers to Lord Shiva had finally been answered. The couple were excited to finally have a child and wanted to bow to the doe in gratitude, but it had already vanished. They wondered if the doe was Goddess Parvathi, who had come in disguise to help them.

As they walked back slowly towards their horses a Yogi appeared out of nowhere.

'Hey Nambi, the child will bring you great happiness. Name her Valli,' he said, blessing the couple and child before departing. Nambi sensed that Valli was no ordinary child, but one blessed by the divine.

Valli grew up under the care of her protective parents and an adoring tribe. The tribe was devoted to their lovely princess and would do anything for her. As she neared adulthood, Nambi began teaching her the responsibilities of a leader. He planned to anoint her as his successor soon, which meant she would be the future queen. She accompanied him to the tribal court of justice to understand and learn the path of Dharma. Nambi took over the entire *Valli Kizhangu* fields from the peasants, as the land was too precious to him, having given him his heir.

He appointed Valli as the caretaker of the Valli estate, instructing her to protect the crops from attack by pests and animals. He also entrusted her with distributing the income generated from the tapioca estate among the peasants. She distributed half the income among them, kept a quarter for herself, and reserved the remaining for emergencies like drought or excess rainfall. It would help to feed the peasants and the poor. Valli became the pride, not only of her father but of the entire tribe.

Valli soon grew up to be an enchanting maiden, admired not only for her beauty but also for her sharp intellect– a rare combination indeed. As tales of Muruga's heroism spread far and wide, Valli found herself increasingly drawn to this man dedicated to upholding righteousness. Contrasting his noble deeds with the greed-driven wars of others, she couldn't help but admire him. Muruga was in her mind all the time.

Rishiraja happened to be at the Valli Estate and found a sculpture of Muruga holding his spear adorned with a garland and flowers at his feet. This could only be the work of someone with great sense of devotion. Rishiraja decided to observe who was behind this act of extreme devotion. Rishiraja left the Valli estate with a knowing smile, convinced of Valli's profound admiration for Muruga.

'Muruga, I have personally witnessed the *bhakti* of this beautiful maiden, she deserves your hand,' said Rishiraja.

Taken aback, Muruga responded, 'O revered one, I am already married. How could I take another wife, it would not be fair to Amrutha.'

'You are not the first one and you will not be the last one. You are a Kshatriya and Kshatriyas always have multiple wives with one being the *pattathu rani, The Queen,*' said Rishiraja.

But...

'Muruga, I have seen so much of the world and I believe in destiny, go and see for yourself, then decide,' said Rishiraja.

Muruga returned to Skandha Kottai. He informed Amrutha of his encounter with Rishiraja and that an important task had been assigned to him. Muruga promised to return soon, and asked her to stay with his parents at Velliangiri. Being a dutiful wife, she wished Muruga good luck, applied a red vermillion on his forehead, and bid him farewell. Muruga mounted his horse and rode away.

After a long ride from Velliangiri, Muruga finally reached Vallimalai. He disguised himself as a hunter to mingle easily with the tribe.

He rode to the Valli Estate, and tethered his horse to a *vengai maram, kino tree.* Muruga noticed a girl standing atop a makeshift watchtower. He wondered if this was Valli. The curiosity got the better of him, and he decided to find out.

Muruga went around the watch tower and looked at the girl standing on it. She looked down to see a handsome young man. Muruga was bewitched, he had never seen someone as beautiful and bright in his life. *'Rishiraja wasn't wrong after all,'* he thought to himself.

'Hey there, who are you? What are you doing here,' Valli inquired.

'I am just a hunter who came chasing a doe,' replied Muruga.

'There is no doe here, you have come to the wrong place. Go search elsewhere,' retorted Valli.

'I have found the doe, I was looking for,' said Muruga nonchalantly.

'Looks like you've decided to get your bones broken. My father and his warriors will be here shortly. If you want to save yourself, leave now,' warned Valli.

'Who are you? Who is your father? And where do you hail from? asked Muruga.

'Hey Stranger, you ask too many questions of a lone girl. Nevertheless, I am Valli, princess of Vallimalai, daughter of the tribal king Nambi. Now leave! she commanded.

Muruga swiftly untethered his horse from the *vengai maram* and rode away. Determined to locate his sculpture based on Rishiraja's coordinates, Muruga began exploring Vallimalai. After few hours of searching, he finally found it and decided to observe Valli from a distance the following day. Typically, the woman of the tribe woke up early, bathed in the nearby lake, and then went to the temple. Muruga found accommodation in Melpadi and set out early in the morning for Valli's Muruga Temple, and concealed himself behind the trees.

Valli, with her hair loose and still damp from her bath, arrived at the Muruga temple. She sat before the idol of Muruga, singing his praises while crafting a garland from the flowers she held in her hand. Once the garland was complete, she draped it around Muruga's neck, then touched her eyes with the other end of the garland. Anything touched by Muruga became sacred to her, she then sat down and started reciting hymns in praise of Muruga, showering Muruga's feet with flowers.

Muruga was mesmerized by what he witnessed. *'Is this how Radha showered her love on Krishna?'* he wondered. Witnessing this display of love, affection, and bhakti all rolled into one, he realized he had never seen anyone so dedicated to him. Rishiraja had been correct about Valli; perhaps, he also knew what destiny had in store.

Muruga decided to test her resolve by devising a small plan. Disguising himself as a *Sivanadiyaar*, a staunch devotee of Lord Shiva, he made his way to Nambi's abode in the foothills of Vallimalai.

'*Thiruchitrambalam, Thiruchitrambalam*,' echoed outside Nambi's home. On hearing this, Nambi came out and encountered a very old man with a flowing white beard and sacred ash smeared across his forehead and forearms. Nambi prostrated before him and invited him inside. Nambi and Kodukkai performed *paatha poojai*, a ritual performed for saints, whereby the couple of the house cleansed the revered one's feet. The *Sivanadiyaar* blessed the couple.

'A*yyane*, can I help you in some way,' asked Nambi reverentially.

'Hey Rajan, I am new to this area. There is a Somanadhar temple in Melpadi; can you provide directions?' asked the Sivanadiyaar.

'My daughter Valli knows all the temples around our town. She will escort you there, and I will arrange for a wagon,' Nambi replied.

Acting as the dutiful daughter, Valli led the old man to the waiting bullock cart. She supported him as he climbed aboard, then boarded another bullock cart as they set off with the clanging of bells around the bulls' necks. Both carts arrived at the Somanadhar temple.

Valli helped the old man get down from the cart and held his hand as they circled the temple and prayed to Lord Shiva.

After sometime, the old man felt tired and dizzy. The old man had not eaten anything since morning. Valli realized that the old man was on an empty stomach. She had packed *thinai maavu, foxtail millet flour,* while leaving her house. She took out the flour, mixed it with forest honey, made small balls out of the mixture, and offered them to the old man. However, due to his trembling hands, they kept falling down. Valli decided to feed him herself. Breaking the balls into pieces, she carefully fed him. While enjoying the food and the maiden, Muruga accidentally swallowed improperly and began to hiccup. Valli held his head in her hand and poured a glass of water into his mouth to help.

After lunch, the old man expressed a desire to perform rituals to Lord Shiva, for which he wished to go to a nearby river. Valli directed him towards the river, which lay close to the forest area, and said that she would wait in the temple while he completed his rituals. This disappointed the old man. He pleaded with her to be kind to an old man and accompany him to the river. Valli confessed her fear of wild animals, especially elephants, which were frequent visitors in the area.

'*Yaam Irukka Bayam Yen*,' said the old man, leaving Valli stunned.

It was Muruga's phrase, famous throughout the land.

Valli agreed to accompany him to the river and travelled together in the same bullock cart, as she was afraid to travel alone. Valli pondered over the phrase the old man uttered and decided to inquire further.

'Dear Sir, where did you learn the phrase, you mentioned earlier?' she asked.

'That's my phrase. Why would I learn it from elsewhere?' retorted the old man.

'It's also used by someone whom I greatly admire,' Valli replied, blushing slightly.

'Ah, a copycat, what sort of a person steals others' phrases? Shame on him,' the old man mocked.

'Mind your words, Sir. He is a divine person, born to protect Dharma and help others,' Valli retorted angrily.

'Who is this unique individual you speak of? It seems someone has fabricated stories, and you, in your innocence, have believed them,' the old man replied sarcastically.

'He is Lord Muruga, commander of the Sura army and scion of Swayambhu, the most revered figure in all of South India,' Valli declared.

'Big deal. Regardless of whether he is a commander or scion, can he save you from trouble right now?' the old man scoffed, laughing.

'Please stop the cart!' Valli commanded the driver.

'I would rather perish in the wilderness than listen to any insults about Muruga,' said Valli, who was now seething in rage.

Not realizing, they were almost near the river now, she jumped out of the cart in a huff and stood away from the old man. The old man finished his rituals and then walked up the bank and came near her.

'Looks like you are a die-hard fan of this Muruga,' said the old man.

'I am not a fan. I am an ardent devotee. Muruga is in my heart and soul,' said Valli closing her eyes.

The old man bought all his fingers together, and pressed them on his forehead, and started concentrating. He had a way to communicate with elephants, a trick he had learned from his brother. Valli heard the trumpeting sound of an elephant and stood petrified. She could see ruffling of trees in front of her. Out of fear, she held the hand of the old man.

'Well, my dear, looks like you prefer me to that Muruga chap,' said the old man with a wink.

'Shame on you! My body, mind, heart, and soul will always be at the feet of Muruga, not with a scoundrel like you. I'd rather be trampled by an elephant,' said Valli with tears in her eyes.

She pushed away his hand and walked towards the charging elephant.

The elephant stopped, turned around, and retreated into the forest. Valli turned to see if the old man had performed some miracle and was shocked to find her beloved Muruga standing before her. Overwhelmed with emotion, she fell at his feet. He lifted her up and embraced her.

Valli was speechless and unsure how to react. After regaining her composure, she withdrew from Muruga's embrace. They left the riverbank and returned home.

Upon seeing Valli with a young man, Nambi grew furious, believing his daughter had sinned and that the man had violated tribal rules. He halted them at the entrance, refusing to allow Valli or Muruga to speak.

'I shall deal with you later Valli, but this man will die in front of you,' Nambi declared angrily.

'Please hear what they have to say before you judge them,' Kodukki pleaded.

'This man deceived us and took our daughter. She probably knew and cooperated, which is treason in our tribe,' Nambi roared.

'Rajan, I am prepared to face execution for treason. If any man in your tribe can defeat me, let him come forward,' Muruga challenged.

'You think you are a great warrior. You will die a dog's death,' scoffed Nambi.

The warriors stepped forward one by one to gain favour from their leader. None of them were even able to string

their bow as Muruga's arrows ripped their homemade bows with speed and accuracy. Seeing this, Nambi decided to face Muruga himself. He fared no better and was quickly defeated. The pride of the hunters was humbled, their heads bowing in shame.

Muruga approached Nambi and formally introduced himself as the commander of the Sura army and the son of Swayambhu. He requested Valli's hand in marriage. Nambi asked Valli if she was willing to accept him as her husband. Overwhelmed, she covered her face and ran inside.

In the evening, Muruga and Valli donned tribal attire, and the witch doctor performed the rituals to seal their union, declaring them husband and wife. After the ceremonies, a grand bonfire was lit, and the entire tribe danced until dawn amidst deafening drumbeats and howls, while feasting on abundant deer and boar meat.

The following day, as per tradition, the bride departed with her groom. Muruga and Valli set off on their horses for Skandha Kottai, which would soon become Valli's new home. Little did she know what awaited her there.

KANAKABHISHEKAM

Riding through beautiful streams and sunlit mountains, Muruga and his new bride reached the Velliangiri hills. Muruga wanted to seek the blessings of his parents and brother before proceeding to Skandha Kottai.

A pleasantly surprised Rishabha welcomed them both. As they touched his feet, he blessed the couple and asked them to wait there, while he informed Shakthi, who could perform *aarthi* before the couple entered the household. Rishabha rushed in to share the good news. An excited Shakthi came running out to greet her son and her new daughter-in-law. She performed the *aarthi* with her close aide and ushered the couple in. Swayambhu was in his private quarters, and the couple went to seek his blessings. He was pleasantly surprised with the traditional tribal dress that his son and daughter-in-law were wearing.

Muruga recounted his chance meeting with Rishiraja and the sequence of events that followed, culminating in his marriage to Valli. Swayambhu told Muruga that meetings with Rishiraja are never by chance; they were smartly planned by him and always produced good outcomes.

Shakthi took her new bride to her private quarters, while Muruga celebrated his wedding by having somapanam with Swayambhu and Rishabha.

'You are so beautiful, my dear!' said Shakthi, taking *kajal* from her eyes and placing it on Valli's cheek.

'You are very kind to me, mother. I don't deserve such praise,' Valli replied humbly.

'You are going to a household where there is already a woman; you need to be amicable with her,' advised Shakthi.

'*Amma*, I am aware of Amrutha. I will forever be indebted to her and serve her,' said Valli.

Shakthi was very pleased to see such maturity from someone so young. She wished her well and placed her hand on her head as a symbol of blessing. Just as the daughter-in-law was having this conversation, Muruga entered his mother's quarters.

'Do you want to stay here with *Amma* for some time while I inform Amrutha, or do you want to come with me right away?' asked Muruga.

'I will do what you want me to do, *Natha*,' said Valli with folded hands, addressing Muruga as her Lord.

'I know you will. I want you to know, you are part of the family now, and I will convince Amrutha,' said Muruga.

'You don't have to convince her. I need her to accept me wholeheartedly. My purpose in life is to serve you both,' said Valli.

Muruga knew of Valli's humble nature even though she was the darling of her father and the Vallimalai tribe. However, Amrutha was a princess and now the daughter of the king of kings. Although it was a norm at that time to have many wives, Muruga knew Amrutha's nature and that she would need time to accept another woman in his life.

'Well, it looks like you have made up your mind to take the bull by the horns,' said Muruga.

'No, *Natha*. I have decided to pay homage to my queen,' said Valli with humility.

Muruga and Valli mounted their respective horses and rode to his abode, which wasn't too far from his father's abode at Velliangiri. Hearing the sounds of horses approaching, Amrutha ran out of her palace to find Muruga arriving with another woman. She was shell-shocked at first but decided not to show her anguish. She knew from their attire that they were married.

Amrutha asked them to wait, went inside and came out with the *aarthi* plate. Muruga's happiness was important to her, and besides, here was a girl who had left her family to come with Muruga as his lawfully wedded wife. Amrutha placed the wet red vermilion on the foreheads of both Muruga and Valli. Valli immediately fell at Amrutha's feet to seek her blessings. Amrutha was taken aback but blessed her, saying '*Deerga Sumangali Bhava,*' which meant, may your husband live long. After all Muruga's life was tethered to Valli too through the holy union of marriage.

The three of them went inside, and Muruga showed Valli to the guest room and asked her to wait there. He went to see Amrutha in her private quarters.

'Amrutha, Rishiraja accosted me and asked me to visit Vallimalai to understand for myself the devotion and dedication of this girl. It was simply overwhelming,' said Muruga.

'Lord, you are a Kshatriya. You are free to marry many women as our custom and law permit it. You don't need to justify anything to me,' said Amrutha, accepting the reality.

'I am not justifying; I am stating the facts. You will also find out soon,' said Muruga.

'You must be hungry after a long journey. I will serve food for both of you,' said Amrutha and stepped out.

Amrutha came out of her quarters to instruct the maids to serve food for them, and there stood Valli in a maid's dress, bringing one vessel after another from the kitchen to serve food. Amrutha was taken aback.

'*Rani,* You and Lord can have food. I will serve it,' said Valli, addressing Amrutha as queen.

'Why are you wearing servant's clothes and doing this work? You are a queen too,' said Amrutha.

'I am no queen. Lord Muruga is my God, and you are his consort. I am eternally your servant, my lady,' said Valli.

Amrutha understood the extent of love and *bhakti* that Valli had for Muruga and for her too. She ran across the room and hugged valli.

'I grew up a protected child and got what I wanted all my life. One thing I dearly missed was having a sister. I finally have one,' said Amrutha, tears flowing down her cheeks.

'I am extremely blessed by your kind words of calling me your sister, my lady. You will always remain my queen,' said Valli.

'If you accept me as your sister, call me by my name and not *my lady*,' said Amrutha sternly.

'It will take me some time, but I will get there,' said Valli.

Muruga came out and saw the bond between his two wives and was pleased.

'There are no accidents or coincidences in life; they are always meant to be. Maybe you two have a karmic connection from the past,' said Muruga.

'A karmic connection that we were sisters from the past and both wanted to marry you,' said Amrutha, laughing.

'Maybe. Quite possible,' said Muruga nonchalantly.

The Muruga household was a bundle of joy, with both the ladies sharing the chores and taking care of Muruga's needs. They knew about the heroics of Muruga in the battle field against Sooran, but they were eager to know about his childhood. Muruga decided that he would rather show them the places than narrate his childhood. It would also serve as a nice vacation with his beloveds.

Muruga first took them to the place where he decided to become a monk as a young boy after he was denied victory. The fight was over a fruit, and hence the place became famous as *Pazhani*. Then they travelled to the place where he played the role of a guru to his own father, teaching him the meaning of the primordial OM. After this act, he became known as Swaminathan, and the place became known as *Swami Malai*. Their next stop was the place where he sat in meditation to Lord Shiva to thank him for the victory. It was here that he prayed for peace, and hence the place came to be known as *Thanigai*.

Valli wanted to see the wedding destination of Amrutha, so they proceeded next to *Thiruparankunram*. Nostalgic memories flooded Amrutha's mind, and Valli teased her about it. From there, they travelled to the place that was closest to Muruga's heart, *Senthilpuri*. The trio spent several days and nights at Senthilpuri, walking, running, and playing in the sand and sea.

The final destination was the place where Muruga played a trick on the poet Moothaati, who was an exponent of the Sangam Tamil language that endeared itself to Muruga. The place was a fruit orchard which had lovely berries that the three of them enjoyed. Valli was so much in awe of this place that she requested they often visit it and also suggested they have a small cottage here. Since the old Moothaati became wiser under the fruit orchard, it became known as *Pazha Mudhir Cholai*.

After enjoying several weeks of vacation, they returned home to Skandha Kottai. It was a long and tiring journey, but extremely fulfilling. As they were about to enter the house, they saw a pigeon on the front door with a message. It was from Deva. An excited Amrutha took the message from the pigeon's legs and read it. Amrutha and Muruga were summoned to Indraprastha immediately. An important event was to unfold, and their presence was required. Amrutha looked at Muruga quizzically, and he assured her that it would all be good news.

The next day, Amrutha got up early and was dressed up to leave, while Muruga was getting ready to leave as well. Amrutha looked for Valli, who was doing gardening in the backyard.

'What are you doing? Get ready, we have to leave,' said Amrutha.

'*Akka*, it's an invitation from your place. It's appropriate that the Lord and you go,' said Valli addressing Amrutha as her elder sister.

'You call me *Akka*, so you are very much part of my home. Now get ready quickly,' said Amrutha.

Valli, who always wanted to make Amrutha happy, never said no to her for anything.

The three of them boarded the chariot. With his two wives behind him, he pulled the horses' reins, which galloped away after letting out a huge neigh. Amrutha told Valli about the people in her household and how excited she was to know what the event was all about. The trio took a short break for lunch and then proceeded to Indraprastha. They reached late in the afternoon.

'Welcome, my dear son-in-law,' Deva said as he hugged Muruga.

Amrutha bent down to touch her father's feet, and Valli followed suit. Deva blessed both of them.

'*Appa*, this is Muruga's wife too, and my dear sister,' said Amrutha.

'Welcome, dear, you are also like a daughter to me,' said Deva touching Valli's forehead.

There was a lot of commotion in the palace, which was decked with beautiful lights, colourful curtains, garlands, and other decorations. Valli had never seen such grandeur before and was observing every little detail. In the massive courtroom were seated all the kings and prominent Sura aristocracy, including Pawan, Prajwal, and Varun. On the other side were seated the great brahmanas, including Prajapathi and Rishiraja. On the throne sat none other than Swayambhu, with Shakthi by his side. Deva, led Muruga and his two wives into the courtroom.

As they entered, rose petals were showered on them by the maids standing on both sides of the red carpet that led straight to the throne where Swayambhu was seated. As Muruga reached the front of the court, just below the throne, he turned around along with Amrutha and Valli and bowed to the august audience in front of him. Amrutha then took Valli along with her to the balcony upstairs, where her mother was waiting.

Swayambhu raised his right hand above his head, and there was pin-drop silence in the court room. He then began to address the audience,

'I am very glad to be in the presence of great kings and learned brahmanas today.'

'We are all present here to witness the passing of the title of 'The Supreme Lordship' to my son Muruga.'

Before Swayambhu could utter the next word, the court erupted with joy. Muruga was the darling of the masses, the pride of the gurus, and the inspiration for all the Kshatriyas. Who better than him to take over the mantle from Swayambhu?

Swayambhu continued,

'When I decided to relinquish the position, I called upon Prajapathi and Deva and sought their inputs.

It was decided we would do something entirely drastic. Instead of the aristocracy alone deciding the supreme leader, we decided to run a survey and ask people from all walks of life.'

'Brahmanas, Kshatriyas, Vysyas, and Shudras all unanimously voted in favour of Muruga. It showed that Muruga was all-encompassing and not viewed only as a Kshatriya. This is a day of reckoning for all of us and probably a foresight into the future,' he concluded.

Prajapathi stepped forward with the palm-leaf manuscript and read out the decree that officially announced Muruga as the Supreme Lordship. Swayambhu then gestured for Muruga to come up the steps and occupy the throne. Muruga climbed the steps and arrived at the throne, turned around, and bowed to the entire audience, who were all screaming '*Aro Hara Aro Hara!*' in unison and throwing flower petals towards the throne.

As per the customs followed at that time, the Supreme Lordship was considered to be the representative of Lord Shiva. Shiva was known as an *abishekapriyan,* the one who accepted everything that his devotees offered by pouring it onto the Lingam. It was decided to perform a symbolic *abhishekam* on Muruga. Here was a man whose birth was destined, who spoke gems of philosophy, was a great warrior and had utmost integrity. Such a person was considered to be like gold, the most precious metal at that time.

Prajapathi on one side and Deva on the other side brought forth two golden pots and poured gold coins over Muruga. The ritual was called *Kanakabhishekam,* a befitting tribute to this wonderful being who paraded the southern part of India in the early part of the Kali Yuga.

As the ceremony concluded, Muruga looked at the audience, his heart filled with gratitude. He knew the responsibility that lay ahead, and he was ready to embrace it with the support of his family and people.

After the formal proceedings, a grand feast was held in the palace courtyard. People from all walks of life mingled, celebrating the new Supreme Lordship. As the night drew to a close, Swayambhu and Shakthi blessed Muruga once more.

'Remember, my son,' Swayambhu said, 'Leadership is not about power, but about serving with humility and wisdom which you have in abundance. You will make us all proud.'

Muruga nodded, understanding the depth of his father's words and the weight of expectation from his father and others.

Under the leadership of Muruga, the land flourished. His reign was marked by wisdom, compassion, and justice. His legacy would be remembered for generations to come.

The story of Muruga became a legend, inspiring many. As long as his story was told, Muruga's name would shine brightly, an enduring testament to the eternal spirit of leadership, commitment, compassion and devotion. Muruga endeared himself to people of all walks of life, hence he would eternally remain in the hearts of everyone till the end of time.

Don't miss out!

Visit the website below and you can sign up to receive emails whenever Arvind Seshadri publishes a new book. There's no charge and no obligation.

https://books2read.com/r/B-A-SKKPC-MSFDF

BOOKS 2 READ

Connecting independent readers to independent writers.

About the Author

I consider myself an accidental author and poet by chance, who found his penchant for words three years ago. I started with a juvenile fiction inspired by my growing up years titled " Tales of Raghu " - Anecdotes of a Madras Boy. I followed that up with a Book on Management integrating Peter Druckers concepts with examples from Mahabharata titled " Peter meets Pandavas " - Management through Mahabharat. My latest release is a Mythological Fiction titled Muruga - The Wise Warrior. It is an attempt to humanize one of the famous gods of South India. The first 2 books are available as e book and paper back worldwide. The new release is available as e book worldwide on Kindle and as a Paper Back in India Besides my books I also published a collection of Tamil Short Poetry titled " ◇◇◇◇◇◇◇ ◇◇◇◇◇◇◇◇◇◇◇◇" as an ebook on Amazon which is available worldwide My literary journey continues as I am working on my next book which is on integrating philosophies from different parts of the world that convey the same message...

Read more at https://www.amazon.com/author/arvindseshadri.